T0348925

LEONTUS

LORD SOLAR

More tales of the Astra Militarum from Black Library

• **MINKA LESK** •
Justin D Hill

MINKA LESK: THE LAST WHITESHIELD
An omnibus edition of the novels *Cadia Stands,
Cadian Honour, Traitor Rock* and several short stories.

SHADOW OF THE EIGHTH
A Minka Lesk novel

• **LUCILLE VON SHARD** •
Denny Flowers

Book 1: OUTGUNNED
Book 2: ABOVE AND BEYOND

SIEGE OF VRAKS
A novel by Steve Lyons

KRIEG
A novel by Steve Lyons

THE FALL OF CADIA
A novel by Robert Rath

CREED: ASHES OF CADIA
A novel by Jude Reid

DEATHWORLDER
A novel by Victoria Hayward

LONGSHOT
A novel by Rob Young

KASRKIN
A novel by Edoardo Albert

CATACHAN DEVIL
A novel by Justin Woolley

STEEL TREAD
A novel by Andy Clark

VOLPONE GLORY
A novel by Nick Kyme

WITCHBRINGER
A novel by Steven B Fischer

VAINGLORIOUS
A novel by Sandy Mitchell

LEONTUS
LORD SOLAR

ROB YOUNG

BLACK LIBRARY

A BLACK LIBRARY PUBLICATION

First published in 2024.
This edition published in Great Britain in 2024 by
Black Library, Games Workshop Ltd., Willow Road,
Nottingham, NG7 2WS, UK.

Represented by: Games Workshop Limited – Irish branch,
Unit 3, Lower Liffey Street, Dublin 1,
D01 K199, Ireland.

10 9 8 7 6 5 4 3 2 1

Produced by Games Workshop in Nottingham.
Cover illustration by Aurore Folny.

See Black Library on the internet at

blacklibrary.com

Find out more about Games Workshop
and the worlds of Warhammer at

warhammer.com

Printed and bound in China.

For Aaron and Fraser. They know why.

For more than a hundred centuries the Emperor has sat immobile on the Golden Throne of Earth. He is the Master of Mankind. By the might of his inexhaustible armies a million worlds stand against the dark.

Yet, he is a rotting carcass, the Carrion Lord of the Imperium held in life by marvels from the Dark Age of Technology and the thousand souls sacrificed each day so his may continue to burn.

To be a man in such times is to be one amongst untold billions. It is to live in the cruelest and most bloody regime imaginable. It is to suffer an eternity of carnage and slaughter. It is to have cries of anguish and sorrow drowned by the thirsting laughter of dark gods.

This is a dark and terrible era where you will find little comfort or hope. Forget the power of technology and science. Forget the promise of progress and advancement. Forget any notion of common humanity or compassion.

There is no peace amongst the stars, for in the grim darkness of the far future, there is only war.

ONE

FORTUNA MINOR, NORTHERN CONTINENT
SEGMENTUM TEMPESTUS
GORROLIS SUB-SYSTEM

The saviour pod slammed into the earth in a spray of dirt and scorched grass, scattering ground-dwelling leporidae back to their burrows in skittering streams as the metal shell bounced clear of its crater. It came to rest with a groan of tortured metal and a fading whine of impotent retro-thrusters.

One of the more curious leporidae, an inquisitive young female, was the first to emerge. It inched forward on long-fingered limbs, snuffling at the air through its octet of furry nostrils as it approached the pod. It fled back to its sanctuary as a glowing orange hole exploded in the pod's hatch, and was hidden back out of sight when the panel was kicked clear by a leather-booted foot.

A lone human emerged from the pod's interior with a long white pistol grasped in one gloved hand, coughing his way clear of the actinic haze of smoke that rose from the crash site. His dark eyes took in his surroundings quickly, from the bare dirt of the saviour pod's impact crater to the meandering wound it had cut into the earth as it came to rest.

The Lord Solar, Arcadian Leontus, stepped down from his fire-scarred transport onto the surface of Fortuna Minor and cast his cold gaze skyward.

Leontus had landed on a high plain of rolling grasses burned a muted yellow by the sun, the open land dappled with patches of shade cast by lazy clouds that drifted across the endless sky. The hills behind him swept up towards a mountain in the distance, a craggy spear of rock that was capped with an unbroken blanket of snow. It could have been serenity itself, were it not for the massacre that painted the vista below in shades of black and red.

Trails of billowing black smoke wove their devastating tapestry across the sky, winding from burning Imperial troop landers as they careened to earth as blazing meteors. Ork aircraft tore at them like pack predators even as they slammed into the warring hordes below, eradicating both black-armoured Goffs and bare-skinned savage orks alike in geysers of fire and churned earth. It was enough to tear the creatures' attention away from their enthusiastic slaughter of their own kind, and the xenos' battle-lust found new targets in the humans arriving in their midst.

Entire wings of Imperial Lightning fighters were swarmed as they fought to defend the fat-bellied landers, but were themselves brought down by scarlet jets that chased their kills all the way to their flaming demise on the endless grasslands below. Several of the ork pilots were so embroiled in the chase that they slammed into the earth beside their victims, refusing to pull out of their dives until their stores of ammunition were spent.

But for each ork craft that was picked off in the swirling dogfights or by the xenos' lack of a self-preservation instinct, still more flew in from the ork-held space port to the southwest, tearing through the Imperial lines to maul the landers with predatory tenacity. Each lander carried hundreds of Astra Militarum troops, if not thousands, and Leontus' mind unconsciously estimated the losses as the doomed vessels ploughed into the earth in mushrooms of promethium flame.

Those Guardsmen that did escape the burning wreckages were set upon by a screaming green tide of orks, who seemed oblivious to the flaming comets that killed them in their hundreds with every impact. Pockets of Imperial resistance fought for survival where they could, but each was slowly overrun by the weight of numbers or by red-daubed vehicles that ploughed through humans and their drivers' own kind with sickening speed.

Leontus activated his helm's vox and listened to the grim chorus playing out across every frequency, each desperate voice begging for direction that might bring order to the disarray. He considered adding his own voice to it, as if his resonant tones might somehow provide a melody for the others to follow back into harmony and perhaps victory.

He killed the vox and cut short the last words of an unknown pilot, ending the doomed woman's prayer before its final affirmation. His voice would change nothing and so did not belong on the already overcrowded vox-channels. Instead, he simply watched and momentarily embraced his isolation.

In the decades that he had commanded the armies of the Segmentum Solar, Leontus had never experienced the scale of defeat that was unfolding before his eyes. He felt the weight of those years bearing down upon him like a physical force, held at bay by a cold, insidious anger that grew with each passing moment. The plan had failed, that much was obvious. There was no hiding from that fact on the bare plains of Fortuna Minor – his political officers wouldn't be able to spin this massacre into a daring victory, nor would the annals of history look upon it as anything but a contemptuous failure. The price of that failure was thousands of lives that he was powerless to save in that moment.

He looked to the skies again with a prayer on his lips, hoping against hope that his last order had been heard and obeyed before his Aquila lander had been shot from the sky and he'd been forced into the saviour pod. His shoulders sagged with relief as he picked out the dark spots on the very edge of the upper atmosphere – Imperial landing craft abandoning their descent and returning to the embattled fleet in orbit before they came within range of the ork flyers. His instructions to call off the attack had been heard, and he thanked the God-Emperor for His mercy.

With the flow of burning landers staunched, he turned his attention to more immediate concerns. It would only be a matter of time before his forces on the plains below were destroyed. Any survivors would make for the defensible high ground offered by the mountain if they had any sense; it was likely that there would be topography there that was more favourable to a man on foot. It certainly couldn't be any worse than the bare ground where he stood.

With the clamour of battle echoing to him over the low hills, Arcadian Leontus turned from the massacre and made towards the mountain.

* * *

'Form up on me! Riders, to me!'

Belgutei let loose a cry of frustration as yet another of his riders was dragged from the saddle by the ork horde, their screams of fear and pain cut short by the hammering blows of brutally primitive clubs and blades. He lashed out at a leering ork face as it came within range of his power sword, the blow driven as much by frustration and anger as by experience. The xenos fell back in a spray of ichor, the body spasming grotesquely as its head bounced away across the bloody ground. Each moment was a maelstrom of snarling mouths beneath hate-filled red eyes, bloodied weapons and screeching horses. Everywhere he looked there were xenos braying for his blood, each hammering heart-beat drawing him closer to the moment he was overwhelmed.

Belgutei wheeled his mount around in tight arcs, driving back attackers that seemed to come from everywhere all at once. He was lost on a roiling sea of green flesh, cast adrift from his riders as they fought their own battles like rocks standing firm against a raging tempest. The occasional whip-crack of las-fire cut through the guttural chorus of screaming xenos, punctuated by the rattling bark of their rudimentary solid-shot weapons and explosive impacts.

His horse bucked beneath him, kicking back to crush the chest of an ork with her iron-shod hooves, then stoving in another's head with her chanfron, the armoured faceplate that protected her head and eyes. Belgutei shouted his encourage-ment with each kick and savage bite, trusting in her armour to keep her safe from the orks' attentions. She was a good horse, Attilan-bred and as battle-hardened as he was, not some show pony from a blue blood's parade ground.

'Good girl, Nomi, keep going!' he cried, gripping the saddle as she rocked violently back and forth. 'Come to us, you bastards, meet your fate!'

The orks surged forward in a sudden rush, propelled by their fellows behind. Belgutei kicked out with a stirruped foot as he fought for room to manoeuvre, smashing teeth from gaping jaws and desperately hacking at bare green flesh with his sword, until he jerked back in surprise as he came face to face with another horse's armoured chanfron – one that he recognised.

'Belgutei,' Do-Song said by way of breathless greeting. The Attilan commander's scarred face was sheened with sweat and spattered with black ichor, but the old man fought with the vigour of someone half his age. His honour guard followed in his wake, snapping off shots with their lasguns and beating back the orks with savage slashes of their swords, and Belgutei realised that the sudden ork surge was less a charge and more a bow wave as they fled before the Attilan horses.

'My lord,' Belgutei said, thrusting down through the skull of a brutish xenos who was trapped between Nomi and Do-Song's horse, Gori. 'It is good to see that you still live!'

'I will ride the winds at the God-Emperor's side, but not today,' Do-Song replied through gritted teeth, his free hand falling to a bloody smear on his abdomen.

'Where is the fleet support, my lord? They were supposed to clear this ground from orbit!'

'Worry later, for now we deal with what is before us,' Do-Song said, kicking out at a charging ork, which fell back with a spray of broken teeth and bloody spit before being beheaded by one of his guards. Like Belgutei, his lance had been shattered in the first charge, but he swung his power-wreathed blade with brutal efficiency to decapitate and maim orks with every strike. 'Gather your riders – we need to break free of this morass.'

Belgutei swung his hunting horn into his hand on the raw-hide cord that hung from his neck, the ancient bone feeling fragile in his adrenaline-fuelled grip. With a quick breath, he let loose a piercing blast through the brass mouthpiece and sounded the muster.

'How can we break free? We have no space to build a charge,' Belgutei said, dropping the horn as Nomi bucked again to kick out at an ork who ventured too close.

'I will make space,' Do-Song said. 'Keep your riders close, Belgutei.'

The first of Belgutei's riders reached him as Do-Song set his own horn to his lips and sounded a long, droning note that fired the blood of every horse and Attilan within earshot. More riders fought their way towards the churning mass of circling horses, regrouping with one another to build momentum and break through to their kinsmen.

'To me! To me!' Belgutei bellowed, looking around for familiar faces amongst the grim-featured Attilans as they began to ride in a widening circle, building pace and rearming their lances in anticipation of what came next. Riders joined the swirling rumble of iron-shod thunder, whipping their reins to join the galloping pace.

Then Do-Song blew on his horn once more, blasting a long, mournful note that carried over the thunder of hooves, and the Attilan charge was unleashed.

Belgutei let out his clan's war cry, a ululating scream that mimicked the lethal scream of the Attilan Raptor Hawk, and Nomi responded with merciless speed. He screamed until his throat ached, until his lungs burned, just as every rider in the charge honoured their kin with their own war cries.

Hateful red eyes flashed past above snarling, sawtooth-filled mouths as the Attilans cut a path through the bare-skinned savages towards a mountain on the horizon, its features hazy and blurred by the extreme distance.

'We make for the mountain!' Do-Song shouted from the very front of the charge. 'We do not falter! We do not slow!'

'*We are with the wind!*' the Attilans chanted in unison.

Then they broke through the mobs of the bare-skinned xenos and slammed into the ranks of black-armoured brutes beyond.

'He's dead!'

Keori Arnetz dragged her sergeant's limp form back towards the burning ork jet, and the line of flaring lasguns that poked out from the crater's lip. Solid rounds buzzed past her head like Death Hornets, but she trusted in the God-Emperor and the orks' piss-poor aim to protect her.

'Arnetz, drop him and run!'

'Frag that!' Arnetz spat through gritted teeth, casting a look back over her shoulder at the other Catachan Jungle Fighters in cover below the dangling tail fin of the downed aircraft. Twenty yards, give or take – it would take less than ten seconds, even with Artova's dead weight slowing her down.

One of the orks mistook her for an easy target, running in close as her back was turned, but it hadn't dealt with a Catachan before. Hearing its heavy footfalls, she dropped Artova and drew her combat knife in a dagger grip, spun, ducked beneath the ork's wild cleaver swing, and rammed her weapon into the creature's gut. The monomolecular edge slid through skin and muscle like a las-scalpel, but a simple gut wound – even a mortal one – wouldn't be enough to put an ork down. That was why she twisted the blade and dragged it upward through the beast's belly and into its ribs, where any sane creature's heart would be, before ripping it clear in a spray of sliced offal and stinking ichor.

The disembowelled ork fell to one side with a moan, clutching at its empty stomach cavity even as Arnetz grabbed Artova's collar and dragged him the last few yards into cover.

'I said the bastard was dead!' Groger yelled between controlled bursts from his lascarbine, as Arnetz rolled their sergeant's lifeless body into the slim protection of the crater.

Though Arnetz was only the squad medicae, it didn't take a chirurgeon to see that Artova was beyond saving. His chest had been caved in by an ork brute carrying a heavy maul made from a Cargo-8's axle, and the second blow had smashed the sergeant's head into bloody pulp.

'You did, corporal. I remember it well,' Arnetz said, ducking as rounds spanked off the dakkajet's scorched hull. 'But I also remember who had the damned vox-codes.'

Arnetz rummaged through the sergeant's pockets for the plastek fob that contained their assigned vox-frequencies. It was smeared with blood, though Arnetz couldn't tell if that was Artova's or that of the dead ork on her own hands. She threw it over to Blasko, the vox-operator, and cleaned her combat knife on the sergeant's trouser leg.

Catachan didn't breed soldiers who were overly sentimental, just effective.

'Give me good news, Blasko,' Groger said.

'Working on it!'

Arnetz checked the charge on her lascarbine and joined the firing line, picking her shots and taking out any orks that looked the Catachans' way.

'Come on, Strukker, what's taking so long?' she called over her shoulder, to where an especially muscular Catachan trooper was siphoning fuel from the downed ork jet into an empty tank.

'I'm not even sure this crap will work,' Strukker said as he shrugged the filled container onto his shoulders and repressurised his heavy flamer.

'Damn it, Blasko, give us–'

'They're ordering a withdrawal!' Blasko interrupted, his vox headset clamped over his ear.

'Withdrawal to where!?' Groger asked, looking at Blasko in shock.

'I don't think it's for us,' Arnetz said, suddenly aware that the rain of troop ships appeared to have halted. She hadn't felt the earth-shaking impact of a crashing lander for a few minutes.

'Fragging cowards,' Groger hissed, coming to the same realisation as Arnetz as he looked to the skies. There was no sign of the fat-bellied drop-ships, and even the Lightning fighters looked to have pulled out.

'Blasko, see if you can raise anyone planetside.'

'We're not forming up for the attack on the space port, so I'm thinking that objective has been scrubbed… No one's got a Throne-damned clue what's going on, but I'm getting a return from a Krieg vox-op about five hundred yards north by north-east,' Blasko shouted.

'A walk in the park,' Arnetz said. Their entire northern flank was filled with a sea of orks and dying Imperials, interspersed with islands of burning scrap that had once been the blessed aircraft of the Navy. If the Krieg were out there, she couldn't see them.

'Does anyone have any better ideas?' Groger asked.

There was no time for anyone to reply. A mob of orks chose that moment to make a run for the Catachans, brandishing improvised weapons and firing their ramshackle guns from their hips as they came. Their fire was indiscriminate, but it forced the Catachans into cover for the few heartbeats it took for the xenos to reach the crater's edge.

Then the orks were in amongst them. Arnetz caught a wild axe-swing from one on her lascarbine and twisted, throwing the blow wide and giving her enough space to blow three scorch-rimmed holes in the creature's bare torso. It did little to slow the beast down and she was forced back a step, only for Blasko to lunge in to slam his combat knife into the ork's eye socket. She emptied the rest of her charge pack at another that reared up behind the vox-operator, blowing out the back of its skull through its gaping maw.

'Hit the deck!' Strukker roared, and Arnetz caught the screech of the heavy flamer's compressor cycling up a heartbeat before she dropped to the blood-slicked dirt.

Heat, unforgiving and primal in its cleansing fury, washed overhead in a tongue of blazing fire. Arnetz felt the sweat on her shaven scalp flash-dry in the backwash, the caked blood on her forearms cracking as the moisture was torn away by superheated air.

Then, as quickly as it had come, the heat was gone. Orks screamed as they burned, their skin blackening and slough-ing from their charring bones as they clawed at their ruined flesh. Strukker grinned at the fruits of his work as his flamer hissed and spluttered, its machine spirit clearly sated by the carnage it had wrought.

'Let them burn!' Groger ordered as the Catachans got back to their feet and collected themselves for the next assault, but the sight of their burning kin seemed to have forced the orks' attention elsewhere.

'Blasko, any Catachan returns on the vox?'

'None, just the Krieg one,' Blasko said, grimacing at the shining burn along his forearm.

'Then we find the blank-eyed bastards and go from there. North by north-east – Strukker, clear us a path.'

Arnetz helped Blasko sling the vox-pack over his shoulder and took a moment to smear a stinking yellow unguent onto his burned arm from a small tin in her medicae pouch.

'Death Hornet honey? Don't waste that on me,' he grunted as Strukker shouldered to the front of the line, cycling up his flamer to fire once more.

'Anything that keeps us in the fight,' Arnetz said with a reassuring slap on his shoulder. 'Now move, trooper. We're not out of this yet.'

Sweat ran freely beneath Belgutei's armoured coat as he rode, down his arm and over the hilt of his sword, mixing with the caked ichor that coated the limb up to the elbow. Each strike tested his tired grip and pushed his fatigued muscles to new, burning heights, but to stop was to die against the black-armoured brutes.

Do-Song's charge had faltered the moment it struck the hulking Goffs – orks clad in black plates of metal that appeared to be bolted directly into their muscular green flesh. The Attilans had carved a path through the savage, unarmoured xenos without much resistance, but they had broken over the Goffs like a wave striking a cliffside. Ogryn-sized beasts smashed aside horses and riders alike with brutal swings of man-sized axes, or tore them apart with vicious chainglaives spewing black promethium fumes that obscured the geysers of blood from their sundered victims.

An ork roared as it advanced on Belgutei, its iron-shod boots kicking up mud as it lunged out of the throng with its cavernous fang-lined mouth ready to bite. Belgutei lashed out and separated the creature's jaw from the rest of its skull, which did little to slow it down. He cried out as the ork's upper teeth sank into his leg, and their eyes locked momentarily. The little red orbs glared from beneath its thick black metal helm, filled with so much hate…

Then its armoured hands grasped Nomi about the neck, and heaved.

The sky and ground whirled overhead in a dizzying arc, with only Nomi's terrified screams giving Belgutei any sense of which way was up or down. He struck the ground with rib-cracking force and rolled, instinctively putting distance between himself and his horse as she clambered back to her feet in a whirl of hooves and cloth barding. She stumbled almost immediately but managed to stay upright, shaking her armoured head as she fought to regain her senses.

His own rise back to his feet was far slower and much more painful; the ork's fangs had made a bloody ruin of his trouser and the leg beneath, and each shallow breath was like inhaling fire into his bruised chest. His sword was gone, leaving him with only his laspistol to defend himself as orks and Attilan riders fought desperately around him.

The ork that had unhorsed Belgutei bulled its way through the fighting towards him, its tongue lolling uselessly over the ruin of its lower face as its blood flowed down the plates of its armoured chest. Taloned hands flexed in black metal gauntlets as a riderless horse galloped past, and Nomi followed it away into the press.

'Go well, my old friend,' Belgutei gasped between agonised breaths, and dragged his laspistol from its blood-slicked holster. His helm came away in his other hand to be held like a buckler, the fur rim and leather strap both wet with his own sweat. Attilan doctrine dictated that a warrior who was knocked from their horse was as good as dead, but Belgutei would not die meekly on his knees.

The ork swiped at him with a taloned hand, then another, each swing clumsy but powerful enough to disembowel him. He met the third with his improvised buckler, the helmet's spiked crown punching through the ork's palm as it was torn from his grip, then fired three laspistol shots at the beast's face.

The ork blocked the shots with an armoured fist, letting out a rhythmic, wet, guttural noise as it pulled the helmet out of its hand just as Belgutei might remove a splinter; the noise it was making was not of pain but laughter, he realised.

He emptied the rest of the laspistol's meagre charge at the ork before his wounded leg gave way beneath him and he fell, with little to show for his defiance but a few scorch marks on its already battered armour.

The creature loomed over him, raising an iron-clad boot as its beady red eyes locked with his.

Its skull disappeared in a blast of ichor and shrapnel as hooves thundered past Belgutei's head, spraying him with mud and the splintered shards of a broken hunting lance.

'On your feet, cousin!' Do-Song commanded, wheeling his horse to face him as his honour guard cleared some space around their leader. He reached out with a hand to help Belgutei to his feet, and it was the last thing he ever did.

Do-Song's chest ruptured in a blur of spinning steel and hot blood, his body bisected by the whirling teeth of a circular saw blade. It tore through his armour, sinews, and bone with a high-pitched screech, spraying his vitae over Belgutei as his torso flopped from the saddle in a boneless heap. His honour guard roared their defiance and charged at the beast that had killed their leader, but Belgutei couldn't tear his gaze from Do-Song's eyes as they looked blindly at the smoke-scarred sky above.

'Belgutei, get up, damn you!'

The voice wrenched Belgutei away from his fallen kinsman. He took Do-Song's power sword from his limp grip and pushed to his feet, taking hold of Gori's reins to steady himself. He dragged what remained of Do-Song's body down and swung himself up onto the blood-slicked saddle, the sword an unfamiliar but comforting weight in his hand.

There were so few riders left, he realised with a twist of grief – less than twenty against the endless ork sea. Hundreds more hulking black-armoured xenos lay between the remaining Attilans and open ground, and the distant mountain that had been Do-Song's last target. With a quick look at the faces about him, Belgutei came to another grim realisation: he was the highest-ranking Attilan left, and his kinsmen were looking to him for leadership as they fought for their lives.

Belgutei took hold of his horn and raised it to his lips. If the Attilans were to die, they would do so on the charge, becoming one with the wind.

Arnetz let out a blasphemous curse as Blasko's eyes unfocused and his features went slack, his usually sun-kissed skin sickly and pale beneath the blood spattered across his cheeks and jaw. A Krieg trooper stepped past the kneeling medicae without a second glance, filling the gap that the fallen Blasko had left in their firing line.

'The vox-set?' Groger shouted, his lascarbine tight to his shoulder as he pumped shot after shot into the xenos.

'Fragged!' Arnetz replied over the whip-crack report of massed lasguns and the braying scream of the ork horde. The brute that had gutted Blasko had smashed the vox to sparking ruin with a single blow, laughing in the face of the Catachan's muscle and training. She snapped off her fallen comrade's ID tag and red bandanna, stowing both in her medicae kit before picking up Blasko's lascarbine. Her own had been cleaved apart by an ork's choppa not long after they'd linked up with the Krieg, and she was glad to have a weapon back in her hands.

The Krieg were suffering terrifying losses with each passing moment; unlike the Catachans, they didn't have the size or strength to meet the orks hand-to-hand, nor could they carve some distance between them and the murderous horde. They fought on regardless, forming ever-shrinking firing lines as they gave their lives willingly to blunt each ork charge. It wasn't a way of war that the Catachans were suited to.

'We can't stay here, Groger,' Arnetz said as she ejected the lascarbine's empty charge pack and slapped in a fresh one.

'I know, I know,' the corporal said, his mouth a grim line as he assessed their options. 'Sergeant Raust, we need to move!'

A Krieg sergeant put down the ork at his feet with a bolt pistol shot, and turned the blank lenses of his gas mask to the Catachan corporal.

'Krieg operational doctrine dictates that we must maximise enemy casualties as we await revised orders,' he said in heavily accented Gothic, before parrying an incoming ork blade on his chainsword. Rough-forged iron squealed and sparked against adamantine teeth as the ork brought all of its weight down on the comparatively slender Krieg trooper, but Raust didn't try to best the xenos in a test of strength. Instead, he put two bolt-rounds into the ork's belly and another into its skull.

'Yeah, that's not happening. We make for the mountain – get clear of these filth and regroup,' Groger shouted over the gunning of the sergeant's chainsword, pointing over the ork mob to the distant cloud-wreathed peak. Raust looked from Groger to the mountain then back again, his expression unreadable beneath his mask.

'Staying here does not maximise enemy casualties, sergeant,' Arnetz added.

'Agreed. Krieg, fix bayonets!'

The remaining Krieg troops attached bayonets to the ends of their lasguns with regimented uniformity, each rank covering the one behind as they paused their fire to rearm.

'Blades!' Groger shouted to the Catachans, who all drew their combat knives and held them ready alongside their lascarbines. 'We make for the mountain. Keep tight and follow my lead.'

A horn sounded nearby, the sonorous note somehow alien to the battle raging on all sides. Arnetz looked to Groger in confusion, but didn't have the chance to voice her question before the Krieg troopers charged forward in a storm of grey greatcoats and volley upon volley of las-fire. Arnetz tore after them alongside the remainder of her squad, cutting, slashing, and shooting her way through the ork lines.

The air was thick with the musty stink of ork sweat and the metallic tang of blood, and she stepped over Krieg bodies as she fought to keep up with the other Catachans. Strukker was at the tip of the spear, his heavy flamer blasting a hole for his comrades to follow as Groger followed on his shoulder to protect his flank.

The horn sounded again, but closer. Arnetz found herself looking around for its source between kills, kicking out at a canid-sized creature with red skin and a maw full of craggy teeth just as the charge collapsed.

A massive ork careened into Strukker from the side, easily half as tall again as the Catachan trooper and twice as broad in its black armour plates. It bowled him from his feet and into a mob of smaller xenos, hefting a maul overhead to deliver a final blow. Arnetz didn't have time to reach her squad-mate and friend, or even to cry out. The ork's maul fell with cata-strophic force, and Strukker's promethium reserves exploded in a blooming geyser of heat and flame. Orks and humans alike screamed in pain and terror as the burning fuel drenched them, splashing across friends and enemies indiscriminately as the fire spread unchecked.

The worst of the explosion was absorbed by the orks between Arnetz and where Strukker had died, but the heat still washed over her in a wave of pain that was as much emotion as physical hurt. She found herself carried forward by the press of Krieg behind, who hadn't reacted to the blast at all – they continued their charge regardless, like servitors who hadn't been given the order to stop.

'Groger!' Arnetz shouted as she stumbled over the scorched carcass of a fallen horse, but the other Catachan was nowhere in sight. She slipped on the horse's spilled innards, which had been torn from its carcass and left the ground slick under her boots, but kept her feet and fought on. There would be time to grieve her squad, but she would have to survive the next few minutes first.

At the head of the charge, the Krieg sergeant, Raust, had taken over as the tip of the spear; his bolt pistol barked without cease, blasting bloody chunks from the xenos as he forged forward with surgical efficiency – until he met a foe whose armour turned aside his fire, and swatted aside his chainsword with the back of a hand. It brought up a heavy glaive and swung wide, felling two of the Krieg troopers ahead of Arnetz as if they weren't even there. Raust caught the backswing on his chainsword and was forced back by the strength of the blow.

Arnetz emptied her lascarbine into the creature's flank, but it did little more than stitch a line of scorch marks into its armour. It ignored her, stomping forward to swing at Raust again and again as the Krieg fought back the orks pressing in from every side. The moment stretched out for Arnetz with every las-shot, each hacking blow, and every body that hit the ground. The air itself resounded with finality – their efforts had fallen short, their disastrous mission ending before it had truly begun. Dead carpeted the ground in every direction, human forms entwined with the orks that had slain them and then been killed in turn.

Raust's pistol clicked as its hammer struck an empty chamber, and the ork's cleaver slammed into his chainsword until the metal splintered and shattered. Adamantine-tipped teeth spewed from the broken weapon as the ork's blade hacked off his arm below the elbow, but the sergeant didn't fall.

Arnetz was running, a bestial scream of her own on her lips as she launched herself at the ork's armoured back. Raust pointed his stump at the ork looming over him, spraying its face with his blood and forcing its next blow wide as he beat at it with the butt of his pistol. Arnetz slammed into the beast, plunged her combat knife down into the gap in its armour between neck and shoulder, and twisted.

The ork roared in rage and pain, grasping at the Catachan as Raust finally fell to his knees and dropped his pistol. Arnetz glimpsed him between the creature's taloned fingers. It was clawing at itself to get to her, leaving scratch marks of bare metal in its own armour as she pulled her blade free and drove it into its bloodied flesh.

Then Raust was back on his feet, the shattered chainblade still screeching in his remaining hand. With a cry, he drove it upwards into the ork's armpit in a spray of ichor.

The xenos brute's strength faltered, and it dropped to one knee as Raust dragged his weapon clear. Like a felled tree, it toppled to the blood-soaked earth next to the Krieg sergeant, with Arnetz still clinging to its back.

Thunder rolled past her in a tide of armoured hooves and slashing blades. She began to crawl over the ork's still-twitching corpse, reaching for Raust as he tried to staunch the flow of blood from his ruined arm. They were alone in the maelstrom, the rest of their people lost to the horde, but Arnetz went to work with mechanical efficiency. The tourniquet she tied was bright red; at first she thought it was blood, then realised with numb detachment that it was one of her squad's bandannas.

'Do you want to die here, Catachan?' a voice asked.

The speaker was an Attilan Rough Rider, bloodied, battered and without his helmet, but still in his saddle despite the wounds he carried.

'Get him out,' Arnetz said, pulling Raust to his feet and pushing him towards the Attilan.

The rider barked an order to another horseman, who scooped up Raust and muscled him into a seated position on the front of his saddle. Then the first rider held out a hand to Arnetz, who took it gladly.

'I am Belgutei,' the rider said, hauling her up behind him.

'Thank you, Belgutei,' Arnetz said, and made to sheathe her combat knife.

'You may need that before we are done here,' Belgutei said. 'Thank me when we are clear of this.'

TWO

Belgutei whipped at Gori's reins as he lashed out with Do-Song's power sword, the blade-heavy weapon growing more comfortable in his hands with each ork he downed. Any adrenaline that had fired his blood was long since spent, replaced by a sense of dislocation that left little space for him to think or plan – there was the mountain and the orks between his soldiers and it. Nothing else mattered.

So the fact that he had stopped in his charge to pick up two wounded warriors was a shock not only to his remaining riders but also to himself. They had been building up momentum for the charge that would see them free of the orks and back on open ground. But he had scooped up the Catachan woman and the wounded Krieg trooper without thinking, arriving too late to assist them in their fight against the largest ork he'd ever seen. Perhaps that was what fuelled his sense of separation from his own body; he had acted on base instinct in that moment, and it seemed like he wasn't alone.

With no humans within reach and with little prospect of making it to the other side of the battlefield, the orks on the northern fringes had long since turned their attentions on each other. Brutally sharp claws and serrated teeth tore into green flesh as improvised weapons bludgeoned thick xenos bones to shattered ruin. They were all easy prey for the Attilans as Belgutei led his riders through the melee, scything down any ork that came too close with heavy swings of his borrowed sword.

'They're turning on one another!' Nomak yelled over to Belgutei, one arm supporting the Krieg trooper who bounced limply in the saddle before him.

'Let them!' Belgutei said.

And then they burst clear of the orks and onto open ground with a cheer that rippled down the line as each rider's horizon became one of rolling hills and open skies, though the latter were still scarred by trails of smoke drifting on the wind. Even the Catachan joined in, hurling curses at the xenos and swearing bloody revenge, but her anger was soon turned on Belgutei.

'Where are we going? Why aren't you turning around?' she asked.

'Because the battle is over. We have lost, Catachan. There is nothing to be gained by doing so,' Belgutei said, and he was surprised to feel cold steel press against his throat in response. A glance downward revealed a muscular arm reaching over his shoulder and a Catachan blade held in blood-caked fingers.

'There are Imperial soldiers back there. Catachans, Krieg, Cadians – hell, there might even be a few of your mob left too,' she hissed into his ear. 'We aren't leaving them.'

It would be the work of a moment to reverse his grip on Do-Song's blade and ram it into her ribs, but something held Belgutei back – something more than the razor-sharp knife held against his throat. He turned his head slowly, wincing as the blade scored a neat line across his neck, and pointed the sword at the other Attilans. There were less than ten riders left, most carrying minor wounds, and it was clear that few of the horses had many miles left in them.

'We are few, too few to help anyone now,' he said carefully, each bob of his Adam's apple grating against the Catachan's knife. 'Besides, we have our own problems.'

He felt the Catachan shift position as she followed the line of his sword to the blur of red kicking up dust to the west.

'Speed Freeks,' she said. She pulled her knife from his throat, and Belgutei breathed a sigh of relief. 'Can we outrun them?'

Gori felt strong beneath him, but he knew her flanks would be frothing with sweat beneath the heavy armour and thick cloth barding. The others' horses would all be the same after hours of charging and vigorous combat, and now their desperate escape, but they were all Attilan purebred and would run until their hearts gave out, if that was their riders' will.

'We can try.'

Belgutei sheathed Do-Song's sword and kicked Gori forward to the front of the Attilan column. Even carrying twice the weight, she was strong, and she reacted to his touch as if they had been bonded far longer than the last frantic hour. Nomak followed with his Krieg passenger, who appeared to be a far more natural rider than the burly Catachan, despite the trickle of his blood that had coated his and Nomak's flanks.

'We have shadows to the west,' Nomak called as he took his position beside Belgutei, seemingly unfazed by the blood that had doused half of his body.

'I have seen.'

'Take this burden and give me three riders,' Nomak said, shaking the Krieg trooper's limp form to emphasise his point. 'I will meet them in their charge and you can make for the mountain.'

'No, cousin. I will not spend our lives so cheaply,' Belgutei said. He had already run through many such strategies in his mind, and discarded each in turn. 'If we turn and fight, we risk drawing more of them in. Our best chance is to make for more uneven ground and hope they lose interest in us.'

'It is a thin hope,' Nomak said, but he slowed to let the others know Belgutei's plan.

'All hope is thin,' Belgutei called after him.

'"Except that which lies with the God-Emperor",' the Catachan said, finishing the quote.

'Indeed. Tell me your name, Catachan, I would know who shares my horse.'

'On the day you might die, you mean?'

'Just so.' Belgutei smiled. He had heard much of the Catachans over the years, of their skill as guerrilla fighters and the living hellscape that was their home world, and was glad to see that their grim reputation hadn't been exaggerated.

'Corporal Keori Arnetz, Catachan Eighty-Third,' she said, shifting her position behind him. 'Do you keep a lasgun on this thing?'

'Her name is Gori, named for the eastern wind,' Belgutei said, reaching down to pass her the lasgun from its saddle-mounted sling. It whined as Arnetz checked the charge and sighted the weapon on the incoming orks.

'They don't look like they're losing interest,' she said.

'They do not.'

Belgutei called out to his riders, asking for speed that he

knew their horses didn't have as they crested the first rise. The orks dropped from sight below the hill for almost half a minute before their ramshackle vehicles ramped over the crest and came down with an almighty clatter. Belgutei watched with his heart in his mouth, hoping that the shearing armour plates and spraying components might slow their pursuers. One machine crashed, an unholy amalgamation of halftrack and dirtcycle, which flipped end over end as its front end collapsed on impact.

His riders cheered, but it was not enough. At least five more of the Speed Freeks' vehicles gouged deep furrows in the earth as their drivers fought for control, but none stopped to aid their stricken comrade. Black smoke belched from their engines as they let out a still-louder roar, and careened up the hill towards the fleeing Attilans.

Even from the front of the column, Belgutei could hear the telltale thud-thud of ork rounds slapping into the ground behind them, and the hollow thumps of shells striking flesh. Dirt sprayed as hard rounds whined past him and Arnetz, kicking up clods of earth that pattered against Gori's armour as she galloped on.

'They're getting closer!' Arnetz shouted and loosed a burst from her borrowed lasgun.

The riders crested the next rise at a far slower pace as the incline ate into their speed, and the scream of wounded horses told Belgutei that he had lost at least one of his men to the orks' indiscriminate fire. There was far less open ground before the next rise, but it was far steeper, and at the top…

A shimmer of golden light in the shape of a man, who disappeared before Belgutei could be sure of what he had seen.

'Who the hell is that?' Arnetz asked.

'I do not know,' Belgutei said, the after-image of the figure still fresh in his mind. The man had looked too small to have been one of the God-Emperor's blessed Adeptus Astartes, but he had no answers to what else it could have been. He erred on the side of caution regardless, ordering his men to be ready for combat as the next climb began.

The hill receded beneath them to reveal an open plain carpeted with sun-bleached grasses and bereft of any trees, bluffs or cover – perfect ground for the orks to catch the riders. But it also revealed the mysterious figure to be a man in a pale blue uniform and golden armour, a long white pistol in one hand and the other held up to halt the galloping riders. Belgutei dragged on Gori's reins as he recognised the figure from the propaganda films, recruitment posters, and statues erected in places of honour on a hundred worlds.

'That's the Lord Solar,' Arnetz breathed.

It was him, down to the golden greaves and the breastplate emblazoned with the Imperial aquila, the flowing red cloak, and the wreathed helm topped with the dawning crest. It was Lord Solar Leontus himself.

Belgutei's riders pulled up behind him, churning up the ground as several horses wheeled about as they fought against their natural instinct to keep running. The others whickered beneath their sweating riders to voice their displeasure as the Lord Solar made straight for Belgutei.

'Lord Solar, you're–'

'Give me your explosives. We don't have much time,' the Lord Solar commanded, making straight for Gori's saddle-bags and pulling the explosive lance-tips clear. 'Catachan, help me – quickly!'

With a confused look at Belgutei, Arnetz slipped down from her perch, grabbed the few remaining explosives, and followed the Lord Solar to a patch of ground a few yards away from the edge of the rise.

'Move the horses away and prepare for a counter-charge,' Belgutei ordered, handing Gori's reins to Nomak as he stepped out of the saddle and took up a bundle of his second-in-command's spare melta-tipped lances.

Nomak did as he was ordered and led the other Attilans away from the edge of the hill, whilst Belgutei followed Arnetz and the Lord Solar to where they were driving the lance-tips into the ground to create a thicket of makeshift mines. He followed their example and worked swiftly but carefully alongside them, the clatter of engines growing closer with each lance they planted, until the Lord Solar stood to look down at the approaching orks. Even with the dirt staining his gloves and the mud caked around his boots and knees, he looked imperious as hard rounds whizzed past or chewed into the crest of the hill.

'Ten seconds – Attilan, get back to your men and charge whatever survives,' the Lord Solar said, stepping back from the edge before breaking into a run. Belgutei found himself dragged back to his feet with surprising strength and pushed into a sprint, just as the sound of ork engines reached a revving crescendo on the incline behind him.

'That's the Lord Solar!' Nomak said as Belgutei swung himself into Gori's saddle, and his second-in-command passed him a primed hunting lance. The Krieg man was on the ground, a borrowed laspistol in his hand as he stood over a prone Attilan rider who had been caught by an ork round and would not ride again. Ahead of Belgutei, the Lord Solar had led Arnetz away from the trap and the Attilans, and they were both taking cover in a shallow depression less than twenty yards from the mines.

'It is,' Belgutei agreed, and he looked around at the handful of Attilans he had left. 'Follow me on the charge and look after each other. We might just make it out of this alive.'

The first ork dragsta crested the hill at a lunatic's pace, the underside twisting through the air as its oversimplified aerodynamics turned its unchecked momentum into a suicidal spin. The driver was ejected as it flipped, the xenos flying clear as its vehicle slammed into the open ground beyond the trap.

Then the other Speed Freeks appeared in a cataclysm of red paint, torn metal and fire.

The bikes were the first to land, the lance-tips impaling engines and riders before blowing both apart with concussive force. Glossy ichor and stringy sinew splashed across the trikes and buggies that followed them into explosive destruction. A second later, the final trukk landed in the centre of the destructive mass and detonated.

Lesser mounts would have reared at the sensory overload, losing themselves to their base instincts no matter what their riders did, but the Attilans did not breed lesser mounts. Gori tensed beneath Belgutei, ready to surge towards the carnage at the slightest command from her rider, trained to harness her adrenaline into devastating speed.

Belgutei didn't need to shout his order. With Do-Song's lance in one hand and Gori's reins in the other, he touched his stirrups to her flank and set her charging into the inferno. His riders followed, directing their mounts into forward motion and onward into the destruction. Scraps of blackened metal landed in their path, embers and butterflies of flaming cloth dancing in their wake as the Attilans charged in to finish off what remained of the Speed Freeks.

To their credit, those orks that survived fought on with burned faces and mangled limbs, hacking at their foes with brutal choppas and firing on horses and riders alike with heavy shootas, but their resistance was cut short by the Attilans' lances. They didn't bother detonating the explosive tips, but ran the creatures through again and again until the beasts stopped thrashing. A blur of gold and blue moved amidst the smoke and burning vehicles with Arnetz at its back, the Lord Solar putting down the orks with clinical cuts and blasts from his legendary pistol.

Finally, once they had all been put down, Belgutei ordered his surviving troops away from the burning vehicles and back to clear ground, the final kills leaving his mouth tasting of sour ash and bitter chemicals. Arnetz met him on the edge of the skirmish, her skin soot-blackened on her arms and cheeks, her borrowed lasgun still in her hands.

'Are you hurt?' Belgutei asked.

'No, I'm… I'm fine,' Arnetz said. She looked back towards where the Lord Solar was approaching a wounded ork, the driver of the first dragsta to make the rise, as it dragged itself away. 'I didn't even know he was part of the first wave with us. Should we…?'

'He can take care of that himself,' Belgutei said. 'See to the others. I will keep an eye on the Lord Solar.'

The Lord Solar drove his sword down through the ork's torso, pinning it to the ground as he primed his pistol. He looked like he was saying something to the xenos as it lashed out at him with taloned fingers, swiping dangerously close to his mud-caked boots.

'What is he doing?' Nomak asked. Belgutei hadn't realised that his cousin had approached – yet another sign that his mind wasn't as sharp as it needed to be. He should have thought of trapping their trail as the Lord Solar had; it was an old trick used by Attilans being pursued behind enemy lines, or to slow fast-moving predators on the steppes of Attila. That he hadn't galled him. Had his own fear blinded him to the opportunity? Or had he been too fixated on their escape to remember that Attilans had more than just simple speed in their arsenal?

'I don't know. Speaking to it, I think?'

Belgutei could hear the harsh rumble of the ork's speech across the open ground between them, and the low murmur of the Lord Solar's response. Then, with little warning, the Lord Solar fired his pistol into the ork's face. There was a blast of heat and vaporised flesh, and the ork went still.

Nomak whistled. 'I don't think he liked what it said.'

'Who did we lose?' Belgutei asked, nodding over to where Arnetz was kneeling next to the Krieg trooper. She hadn't moved the prone Attilan, which he took as confirmation that the rider was dead.

'Almost everyone,' Nomak said. He was looking in the opposite direction, down onto the plains below, where a sea of green orks screamed war cries that could still be heard on the wind, though now only faintly.

'I need your mind here, Nomak, not back there on the plain,' Belgutei said. 'We're all tired, all dulled by what we've been through today. The more eyes I have looking forwards, the better chance we have of making it through this alive. Now, who do we have left?'

'Just you, me, Rugen and Csaba. Utari was dead when we pulled her from the saddle.'

Belgutei twisted around and took in the two Attilans that remained, each leading a riderless horse behind them. Bile rose in his throat at the thought of how many riders had been lost, the friends and comrades who he had known since their days amongst the hunting lodges of his home world.

'Four of us?' Belgutei breathed. 'We landed with more than five hundred.'

'Maybe others escaped? We can't be the only ones who got away.'

It was a fool's naive hope, but Belgutei found himself praying for the strength to believe.

'I've heard stories of the orks taking captives before,' he said. 'Maybe, in the God-Emperor's mercy...'

He looked to the plains, at the mass of orks that roiled between the burning landers, and spat bitterly in the dirt. A horse nibbled at a patch of ground on the hill below, the remains of an Attilan rider slumped in its saddle. He recognised Battari's steed by the devices woven into its barding, the emblems of the hunting lodge that had bred him for war. Little was left of Battari himself above the waist, just a ruin of red meat and shattered bone from the orks' heavy guns.

Belgutei found himself unable to look away, numbed by the sight of his comrade's broken body. He had known the man for years, and charged into battle at his side more times than he cared to remember. Now all that remained of his worldly flesh wobbled in the saddle as his horse tore clumps of dry grass from the earth with its teeth, awaiting directions from its master – directions that would never come.

How many other horses had been left riderless in the last few hours? How many men and women were little more than cooling meat beneath a foreign sun?

'We need to move,' the Lord Solar called out as he approached. His pistol was still clasped in one hand, the other pointing to the plume of smoke rising from the destroyed ork vehicles. 'That will be visible for miles in a matter of minutes. I will need to borrow a horse.'

'Of course, my lord,' Belgutei said, tearing his eyes from Battari as he searched his memory for the proper honorifics. He'd never even met a planetary governor before, never mind someone who commanded the armies of an entire segmentum. But if he'd used the wrong titles, the Lord Solar gave no sign, and Belgutei made off towards where Arnetz was tending to the Krieg trooper. His own leg was throbbing where the ork had sunk its fangs into him, and the bloodstained fabric felt worryingly hot under his touch.

'Nomak, get Battari's horse and give it to the Catachan woman, Arnetz. The Lord Solar can ride Utari's,' Belgutei ordered with a sigh, turning Gori from the plains and back towards the mountain. 'If the Krieg can ride, then he rides with Arnetz. We have carried him far enough – we stopped for him once already, and I won't have him slowing us down.'

THREE

Leontus led the others away from the still-burning ork vehicles towards the mountain, forgoing any reminders to keep their eyes open on the unfamiliar terrain. They were all on edge; that much was clear from the wary glances cast back on the plains and the hands that rested close to their weapons as they rode.

Leontus rode at the front of the makeshift column alongside the Attilan sergeant. The position served a dual purpose: firstly, he was ideally situated to see the ground ahead and to deliver orders to the riders. Secondly, and perhaps most importantly given the ordeal that they had suffered on the landing fields, he was visible to almost all of them. They could put their trust in him to lead them to safety – or at least what might pass for safety on a barren agri world infested by orks.

The sergeant, who had introduced himself as Belgutei, hadn't argued with Leontus' orders to send a rider ahead to scout the trail. That suggested the man had a sound tactical mind, though it could also indicate that Belgutei feared to challenge a superior officer's orders in spite of his own instincts. In either case, Leontus knew he would need to get the measure of the Rough Rider if he was going to be able to make use of him.

More concerning was the greyish pallor that had begun to take hold over the Attilan's rough and weather-beaten features, and the glazed look that he fought ever harder against the further they rode into the craggy foothills. The man was clearly suffering the effects of blood loss or shock, or perhaps both. Until they found a safe place to make camp, he would have to ride on, but Leontus knew enough of Attilan stoicism to trust him to stay in the saddle.

Of the other Attilans, there wasn't much to say. Each was a hard-faced killer, toughened by a life spent in the saddle riding down the enemies of the God-Emperor. They all nursed minor wounds, and more than one of their mounts looked to be in need of attention, but they hadn't questioned Leontus when he'd been given their fallen comrade's horse. That showed at least a modicum of restraint, if not respect.

The Catachan medicae, Arnetz, rode at the very end of the column, ahead of their rearguard. She wasn't a natural rider, an issue compounded by the near-dead weight of the Krieg sergeant who shared her saddle; he was drifting in and out of consciousness now, and was evidently the source of the bloodstain that half-covered Belgutei's scout before he had galloped ahead.

'You see something, my lord?' Belgutei asked, turning to face where Leontus was looking.

'No, just taking in our forces,' Leontus said, ignoring the slight look of surprise on Belgutei's face at his use of the word *our*. 'I did not expect to see non-Attilans amongst you. That you chose to rescue a medicae was a perceptive move.'

'I… I did not plan it,' Belgutei said, turning away from Arnetz with a shake of his head. 'They showed great bravery in killing an ork, one of the largest on the field. It would not have felt right to leave them there, my lord.'

'That is reason enough. They will be useful,' Leontus said, and pulled on the reins of his borrowed mount to turn her aside. Her name was Nashi, and she was far less responsive to his commands than his own horse, but that was hardly surprising given that he'd had decades to bond with Konstantin and only a matter of hours in Nashi's bloodstained saddle.

The path they had taken into the craggy foothills of the mountain was winding and circuitous, designed to help mask their tracks and lose any pursuers in the tight rocky crevices that weaved through the landscape like rainwater on glassaic. They had lost sight of the massacre at the landing site not long after Leontus had joined the Attilans, but the after-images still lingered at the forefront of his thoughts the same way a tongue always finds a loose tooth.

There were questions that would need to be answered, but they would have to wait.

Leontus raised a hand to their rearguard, a young Attilan who trailed a few hundred yards behind the main column, and relaxed a little when they raised their hand in return. Still no sign of pursuit, which meant the orks' focus hadn't strayed far from the landing fields. That boded well for Leontus and his little warband, but not for the sorry souls who had been caught up in the massacre.

Once back at the front of the column, Leontus found Belgutei examining the walls of the next crevice. He trailed a bare hand across the grey-and-white pitted stone, then sniffed at his fingers before reaching down to tear free a clump of mottled green moss from a fissure in the rock.

'What have you found?' Leontus asked.

'The ground is spongy here, the rocks smoother at ground level. And look here, moisture clings to the wall,' Belgutei said, holding out his hand to show the water glistening on his fingertips. 'We are nearing a water source. It would be good to rest there awhile, cool the horses and see to their wounds... And our own.'

Leontus nodded as Belgutei's hand drifted down to his blood-stained thigh, and the Attilan let out a soft breath as he pressed the cold moss against the wound.

They followed the path of the crevice floor around a twisting turn, then rose up a short shale incline to find Belgutei's scout waiting for them at the top. His horse was dripping wet, and his features were split by a wide grin.

'Belgutei, my lord,' he said in heavily accented Low Gothic as he nodded to each of them in turn. 'It seems our luck is turning.'

Leontus looked out over a vast lake, its waters rippling in the cool wind that drifted down from the mountain. The peak's looming, sentinel-like presence was far closer now, its ragged edges having grown sharper as they lost the haze of distance. Its summit was lost behind dark clouds that promised rain where they were split by the snow-blanketed shoulders of the mountain and the glacier that Leontus supposed must be somewhere beyond.

He rode alongside Belgutei to the water's edge, but neither gave the order for the other riders to come forward.

'Did you check the water, Nomak?' Belgutei asked his scout, resting his hands on the pommel of his saddle as he looked out over the lake.

'Taku walked straight in. I trust his nose,' Nomak said, slapping his horse's neck affectionately.

Belgutei said something in guttural Attilan that robbed Nomak of his self-satisfied smile.

'Arnetz, do you have a water kit?' Leontus shouted. The Catachan passed her horse's reins to another rider, then slid from the saddle and made for the lake's edge, pulling a small plastek phial from her bag. She returned a few moments later, the phial filled with a faint pink liquid.

'Microbial contamination, my lord,' she explained, holding up the plastek tube to the light. 'It's not safe to drink, for us or the horses.'

Though they showed no outward sign, he knew that this news would be another unwelcome blow to the Attilans, more so for the effect it would have on their mounts than themselves.

'Xenos taint perhaps?' he asked.

'Unlikely, the markers would be different,' Arnetz replied. Belgutei held out a hand and she passed him the phial to examine. He tossed it to Nomak a moment later, glaring at the younger rider as he turned his horse reluctantly from the shore.

'Standing water, then,' Leontus mused aloud, raising himself in his saddle to take in the lake's surroundings. 'But where there is water, there is a source...'

The lake stood on a natural plateau, overlooking the western, southern, and eastern approaches to the mountain, and its waters must have created the maze of crevices in the surrounding topography over thousands of years of flooding and refilling. To the north, where the plateau met the base of the mountain, he could just make out a point where the surface roiled and foamed beneath a dark void, and he thanked the God-Emperor under his breath.

'All of you, follow me,' he ordered, then set Nashi off at a reluctant trot to the north. She was more stubborn now the water was within sight, but he pulled her away sharply each time she made to head for the lake. The others had similar issues, but were able to master their mounts with a lifetime's experience; Arnetz was less successful, and more than once she had to wrench at the reins to keep her horse from drinking.

Fortuna Minor's sun was nearing the western horizon before they reached the lake's northern edge, and the point where meltwater from the mountain ran into it via a wide channel. The river's source was further to the north, and Belgutei sent Nomak ahead once more to scout the ground in the hopes that it would be less tainted further from the lake.

'What are you hoping to find, my lord?' Belgutei asked.

'Somewhere that we can rest out of sight of the orks. Something defensible,' Leontus said, pointing up the river to where Nomak lingered on the threshold of a slot canyon cut through the sheer rock of the mountain, the water sloughing around his horse's hooves as he led the way into the half-lit interior.

The river had pierced through layers of dark volcanic rock through thousands of years of erosion, its walls slick with moisture and thick with plant life. The canyon's roof was a tangle of looming stone and dangling roots, resembling the stooping claustrophobia of a forest canopy cast in dead stone. They followed the twists and turns the water's path had carved all the way to its source: a void-black cavern, a bleeding wound in the foundations of the mountain. The cavern's mouth was almost as wide as the canyon, large enough for mounted riders to enter three abreast without their helms touching the ceiling.

'Nomak, Rugen, take a look. The rest of you be ready,' Belgutei said gruffly, looking pointedly at Arnetz as she tried to keep Sergeant Raust upright in the saddle. The two Attilans nudged their horses forward and disappeared into the gloom, leaving the others in a tense silence that was broken only by the babbling hiss of the river.

Less than a minute later Nomak reappeared, lumen in hand as he waved for the rest to follow him.

'It's clear, Belgutei, as far as we can see.'

Leontus followed behind Belgutei as he trotted forward into the darkness and the cathedral-like space beyond. Nomak lifted his lumen-stick and held it above his head, illuminating the high ceiling and the tool marks gouged into the stone by ancient miners who had long since abandoned their work. His light barely grazed the very tips of stalactites that hung down from the distant ceiling, high enough that a Warhound Titan could walk beneath its eaves without risking its paintwork.

The waters had worn a path through less than a third of the space, creating two large pools that fed the river beyond with a constant flow from deeper in the chamber, where a higher mezzanine-like level created a twenty-foot-high waterfall.

'This will do,' Leontus said to himself. He dismounted and walked to the rear of the massive chamber, past the largest of the two pools of water, to where a short slope of stacked stone led up to the higher level. There were no signs of life there – no orks or predators that had made the cavern their home. Just slick rock and shadows, untouched by light for only the God-Emperor knew how long.

It would serve his purposes perfectly, at least for now.

He turned back to the centre of the cavern and looked over his meagre forces: four Attilans, a Catachan, and a badly wounded Krieg. They were all tired, bruised, and afraid as they looked up at him – a far cry from the thousands of troops he should have had at his command, each a nameless face on the parade ground but for the workings of circumstance.

But they were alive and at his side, which made them invaluable.

'You have all worked your own miracles today,' Leontus said, his voice echoing over the burbling hiss of the river as he strode back down to the cavern floor. 'You survived a massacre that should have seen each of you dead a hundred times over, and fought your way clear. You had the strength and the faith to follow the path that the God-Emperor set before you, just as He set mine before me. Tomorrow, we will see where His vision takes us, in His name and for His glory. But tonight we make camp here, bind our wounds, and give the horses some time to rest.'

Belgutei glanced over to his riders, who hadn't moved to dismount despite Arnetz and Raust both stepping down from their saddle with difficulty. The Attilans all looked from the Lord Solar to their sergeant, clearly thinking the same thing.

'My lord, I must ask you to reconsider,' Belgutei said carefully, wincing as he shifted his weight in his saddle. 'If the water's good, we should let the horses drink and move on – we are still too close to the orks to make camp.'

'There is good, dense terrain between us and the orks, and it's unlikely that we'll find a position as defensible as this one before nightfall. Besides, the horses are tired and several of you have wounds that need attention – including you,' Leontus said. 'So we make camp here tonight.'

The Rough Rider would make a poor politician, that much was clear. He wore his thoughts on his face far too openly, and Leontus could almost read the man's reluctance even as he nodded and barked an order to his men in Attilan.

They dismounted at his order, and began to make camp as Leontus stepped forward to help Belgutei down from his saddle, then supported him as he led him over to the closest pool. Leontus glanced towards the cave entrance, where Arnetz was crouching by the river's edge with another plastek phial in her hand. She was close enough to hear their exchange over the rushing of the water, and looked unrepentant as Leontus beckoned her over.

'Is the water cleaner here?' he asked.

'Perfectly drinkable, if a little high in some mineral content, my lord.'

'Good. See what you can do to triage these wounds, Arnetz. Start with Sergeant Belgutei here.'

'But my lord, Sergeant Raust–'

'If Sergeant Raust hasn't bled to death already, then he will keep a little while longer,' Leontus said, more coldly than he had intended. He looked over to where the Krieg sergeant sat in a dark corner of the cavern, his eye-lenses staring out blankly towards where the Attilans tended their horses. 'I will assist you with Sergeant Raust later, but I need Belgutei back in the saddle as soon as possible.'

'He is not what I expected,' Belgutei said as Arnetz cut away the bloody fabric of his trouser and peeled the sodden cloth away from the torn flesh beneath. It drew a hiss from the Attilan, but he remained mercifully still.

'What did you expect?' she asked. She pulled a portable lumen from her bag and gave it to Belgutei. 'Here, point this at your leg. Contrary to popular belief, we Catachans can't actually see in the dark.'

'I don't know. A soft-world politician maybe, or a tender-handed Administratum clerk. He is more like a commissar.'

'I've heard he spent time in the scholams in his youth,' Arnetz said, looking over to where the Lord Solar was organising the Attilans to search the rear of the cavern for other exits, and setting a watch on the cave mouth whilst he and the remaining Rough Rider saw to the horses. 'A good job he isn't a commissar, though, else I think he'd have shot you for questioning an order.'

'Give him time.'

With the caked blood wiped away and the light in place, she examined the wounds on Belgutei's leg. Each was a couple of inches deep, the edges torn as if by a serrated edge.

'You were bitten? I'm only seeing a top set of puncture wounds – was your horse caught too?'

'I don't think so, but Nomi ran away not long after that, so I can't be sure,' Belgutei said.

'Nomi?'

'My horse. The grey is Gori, she belonged to my captain.'

'I'm sorry,' Arnetz said, noting the Attilan's use of the past tense. 'Perhaps you'll find Nomi again before this is over. Dare I ask what happened to the ork?'

'I took away its lower jaw, but the bastard tried to bite my leg off anyway,' Belgutei said.

Arnetz wasn't surprised. She'd gutted, stabbed, and shot more orks in the last day than over the years she'd spent on campaign across the sector, and not one had gone down easily. They seemed to resist death by sheer force of savage will. At least on Catachan the local predators had the sense to know when they were dead.

Thoughts of home gave way to her last sight of Sergeant Artova, his skull crushed to bloody paste. Blasko cut nearly in half by a brutal ork choppa, and Strukker's final moments as the flames consumed him. Fellow Catachans she had known and served alongside for years, all dead because...

'Arnetz?'

'Sorry, just... thinking for a moment,' she said, turning away from where Leontus was soothing a fussing horse. 'I'll have to use some counterseptic on the bites to prevent infection, but you'll have to keep them clean.'

Again the Attilan grunted in response, and Arnetz suspected that now their hurried flight was over, he was beginning to process the day's events. She'd seen it before, even amongst the most hardened warriors after a fight they were lucky to survive. The vacant stares and monosyllabic responses were the most common and least destructive of the symptoms, but it was a slippery slope.

Belgutei let out a hissed curse as she shook the counterseptic onto the bites, the white-grey powder turning a deep red as it absorbed the pooling blood and brought his mind back to the moment.

'Dwell on the past later, Belgutei. Your men still need you if they are to survive.'

'Survive?' Belgutei said with a derisive snort. 'I led them from a quick death to a slow one.'

With quick, percussive snaps Arnetz pulled each puncture closed with staples, then bandaged the wound tightly. Hopelessness wasn't an emotion that she could empathise with – her upbringing had seen to that. On Catachan, she had learned that there was always something that you could do if you kept your wits. There had been times where she had felt a bone-deep melancholy, just as any other person might, but her body had its own will to survive, and the long-learned muscle memory took over in those moments. Her people were survivors above all else, and she would do all she could to keep going and to keep those around her alive.

'You gave them life, Belgutei. Now you need to make sure they do something worthwhile with it,' she said as she tied off the end of the bandage and packed away her kit. She wanted to be away from the Attilan, from the aura of despair that surrounded him alongside the stink of horse sweat and counterseptic. She needed fresh, open air – to be surrounded by something other than stinking horses and cold, moss-covered stone. It was a need she had felt since she had left Catachan, when she had first experienced days of confinement in sterile corridors of plasteel and adamantine rather than the oppressive and deadly abundance of life on her home world.

No one tried to stop her as she stepped into the shadows near the cave mouth and left the claustrophobic darkness behind for the canyon, where whispers of light still shone through the tangle of stone above. Cold air buffeted her, stinging her bare arms and shoulders as the mountain wind sprayed droplets of icy water across the cave mouth. It felt good. It reminded her that she still lived, despite every experience of the last few hours that should have seen her dead along with all the rest. She inhaled cool breaths, so different from the dense humidity of her home world, and drew on old habits in an attempt to clear her mind.

First she cleaned her knife in the river, noting the new nicks on the blade's edge as she scrubbed dried xenos blood from the blue-grey steel. Next, she took inventory of her medical supplies, which had been badly dented since the landings; she made a note to see what the Attilans had stashed in their saddlebags to replenish her stock of bandages and counterseptic powder.

'It was you who killed the big one,' a voice said from ahead, heavily accented with throaty Attilan consonants and an extended sibilance that was unique to the speaker. A Rough Rider knelt in the lee of the cave wall, all but hidden in shadow as river water speckled his coat.

'Heard the others talking on the ride,' the man said. 'You killed the xenos general, or whatever passes for a general amongst the orks.'

'They call them bosses,' Arnetz said, her attempt at still-ness slipping away like water through cupped hands. 'And he wasn't the warboss.'

'Oh yeah? How do you know that?'

'Because I've seen a warboss before, and it was twice the size of that beast we put down,' Arnetz said. 'Do you have any wounds that need tending?'

'Nothing that won't heal in time, but thank you. I would not want you to waste what supplies you have left on the likes of me.'

'I wouldn't call it a waste if it keeps you in the fight.'

'I think that our fight is done, Catachan.'

'If you've got breath left and a working trigger finger, you're still useful to the God-Emperor.'

'Quite so.' The Attilan chuckled and stepped out of the shadows clinging to the cave's walls, revealing himself to be much older than the other riders. His upper lip was twisted around a deep scar that bisected his long moustaches and revealed the lho-yellowed teeth beneath.

'I am Rugen,' he said.

'Arnetz,' she replied, and shook Rugen's offered hand.

They both turned as the Lord Solar called for her from back within the cave.

'I think you are needed,' Rugen said, releasing her hand.

With one last breath of the open air, Arnetz left the Rough Rider to his watch and moved back into the cave.

'What did you find?'

Arnetz kept her head down as she worked to clean and close a long cut across the Attilan youth's ribs, pinching the sides of the wound together as she waited for a chem adhesive to take hold. Her patient had returned from the rear of the cave shortly after Arnetz had taken a moment outside, and he was relaying his findings to the Lord Solar as she worked.

'There is nothing up there, my lord,' the Attilan said through gritted teeth, turning his head away from the odour of chems and melting flesh. 'We found three passages. Two were dead ends, and the third is impassable because of the river.'

'Would it be possible to get in from the other side?'

'No, my lord. The water has filled the chasm, and no man I know could hold his breath to swim it.'

'Very good. At least we only need to watch the one doorway,' Leontus said with a smile, which the young Attilan returned. 'Get some water and rest, Csaba. You have next watch after Rugen.'

The rider beamed with pride at the Lord Solar's casual use of his name, and made the sign of the aquila as he was dismissed.

Arnetz washed the blood from her hands with water from her canteen, but there was no way for her to scrub everything clear. The risk of infection was high with all battlefield triage, but gangrene tomorrow was preferable to a corpse today, as the old saying went.

'You know their names,' she said eventually, when it became clear that Leontus wouldn't leave without a reply.

'I do. I have spoken to each of them,' Leontus said, his dark eyes roving over the Attilans as they washed the sweat from their horses with helmets full of water, or tended to wounds too minor for Arnetz's time. 'The only person I haven't spoken to yet is you.'

She fought down the cold twist in the pit of her stomach. An audience with the Lord Solar would have been unthinkable only a few days before; for Leontus to simply be in the presence of all Astra Militarum forces in the Segmentum Solar was a fool's ambition. She'd known hardened veterans still tell the stories of how they'd caught a glimpse of him on parade, or once breathed the same air as the greatest living exemplar of the Imperial Guard. There was already talk of his being sainted one day – to be spoken of in the same breath as Macharius – but she considered such concerns to be well above her pay grade.

'I need to see to Sergeant Raust before the light fails, my lord.'

Arnetz gathered what remained of her medicae supplies and made towards where the Krieg man still sat, his chest rising and falling in shallow pulses beneath his respirator pouch.

'He's lost a lot of blood,' the Lord Solar said from her side. Raust made to stand at the Lord Solar's approach, but he put a hand on the sergeant's shoulder and told him to be still. She was aware that he had followed her to Raust; his armour gave off a soft glow in the gloom, shining like a beacon that made him all but impossible to ignore.

'It looks like a straightforward amputation. I'll get you cleaned up, and you'll be back to fighting fit in no time at all,' Arnetz said, dropping into a squat beside Raust's mangled arm. Under her lumen's cold light, the wound looked as black as the stone on which he lay, the ragged edges crusted with dried gore and scraps of dead skin, whilst the centre still seeped dark arterial blood despite the tourniquet. She felt the Lord Solar's eyes on her as she examined the savaged limb, the weight of his attention unwelcome as she thought about how best to dress and disinfect the injury.

It was a lie, of course, but one that came easy to medicae-trained troopers across the galaxy; she had to reassure her patient, even if the best she could offer him was a less painful transition from this life to the next.

'You should conserve your supplies, Corporal Arnetz,' Raust

said, his voice muted by more than just his respirator. 'To waste any of our limited resources on me is–'

'My decision,' the Lord Solar cut in, though his harsh tone was softened by the warm smile creasing his features. 'To give up on one-sixth of my forces on a whim would be incredibly short-sighted, don't you think?'

'I must protest–'

'Corporal Arnetz?' the Lord Solar prompted. She stood and moved out of earshot of Raust, followed by Leontus.

'The wound is treatable, but I'm a medicae, not a miracle worker,' she said reluctantly. 'I can patch him up, but the risk of infection is high. He needs a chirurgical team with a fully stocked and sterilised theatre, and we have neither.'

'What *do* you have?' the Lord Solar asked. He unclasped the Radiant Helm and slipped it off, his short-cropped dark hair slicked to his head by sweat.

'Some sachets of counterseptic, a couple of scalpels, tweezers, bandages, a surgical stapler for larger wounds, and a needle and thread for when that runs out,' she said, rummaging through the bloodstained interior of her medicae bag. 'A couple of syrettes of anaesthetic that'll take the edge off the pain, and a laspistol for when the pain is too much.'

'We'll leave the laspistol for a last resort,' the Lord Solar said with a grim smile, pulling off his gloves and placing them into his helm. 'Would it help to have a second pair of hands to assist you?'

'Of course, my lord,' Arnetz answered, and was more than a little surprised when the Lord Solar simply nodded instead of calling over one of the Attilans. 'Are you medicae trained?'

'Something like that.' He gave a faint smile. 'I'm at your disposal, medicae.'

'Thank you, my lord,' Arnetz said, the cold twist in her

stomach returning at the thought of directing the Lord Solar. 'We'll get started as soon as you've cleansed your hands – there are some sterile gloves in my bag that you can use.'

She returned to Raust's side as the Lord Solar made for the riverside, and took the opportunity to take another look at the Krieg's arm. She studied the wound intensely, visualising how it could be repaired and what flesh would need to be cut away, and noted the strange, musty smell that had settled around Raust. Beneath the coppery sharpness of his blood, he smelled of dust and stale air, like a room that had been locked for years and only recently rediscovered.

Arnetz was slipping on one of her few pairs of thin rubber gloves when the Lord Solar returned, and she passed him a spare pair to put on as she set out her supplies within easy reach.

'Once you've got those on, get a syrette of pain blocker ready and bring the light closer, my lord. I need to see.'

Arnetz worked methodically on Raust's arm. The Lord Solar looked on, assisting her as she directed but remaining otherwise silent as she cut away the scraps of dead flesh clinging to the ragged wound.

Raust displayed all the stoic fortitude that she expected of a Krieg trooper. The only sign of discomfort he betrayed was a tension in his uninjured limbs – an admirable level of stoicism, but not one that he could maintain for long. She asked the Lord Solar to administer the first dose of pain blockers after a short while, and Raust slipped into unconsciousness not long after that.

That left her free to focus on her work, rather than being reminded of the pain she was inflicting. The Lord Solar soon faded from her attentions too; he was just another assistant helping her to save the life of a comrade, though Rugen and Nomak's not-so-subtle attempts to watch the improvised surgery threatened her concentration more than once.

'Good thinking with the tourniquet,' the Lord Solar said as she cut away at the torn muscles around Raust's shattered forearm. 'You likely saved his life with that.'

'Thank you. They work in the short term, as the oxygen-starved tissues below the tourniquet will eventually start to die. We're trained to loosen them every thirty minutes to preserve the flesh, when we can,' Arnetz said. She knew that her words were defensive, but her pride wouldn't allow her to remain quiet.

'That's good,' the Lord Solar said. 'It's very rare that I watch a medicae at work, but it's good to see that your training was so comprehensive. We should always look for ways to improve survival rates.'

'More chirurgeons on the front lines, maybe?'

The Lord Solar let out a snort of laughter. 'Perhaps. Or perhaps a change in tactical doctrine is in order – I've known many generals who ignored their attrition rates in pursuit of arbitrary objectives. I've inherited more than one such disaster.'

Arnetz raised an eyebrow at that, her eyes flicking away from the clamped vein between her fingers to the Lord Solar's features. His dark eyes met hers with cold intensity. Her cheeks burned with sudden heat, as if she were a child caught doing something she shouldn't be.

She swallowed. 'Such words would see someone of my rank shot for insubordination.'

'A good thing that I am not your rank, corporal,' the Lord Solar said in a low voice, any threat in his words disarmed by a thin smile. 'But one would be excused a dark thought after the events of today.'

'My lord, I–'

'Ill intentions fester, like wounds that are left untreated, and will leach poison into the blood and the mind,' the Lord Solar said, nodding to the vein clamped between Arnetz's bloodied fingertips. She returned her attention to it, pulling a suture tight in a practised flicker of movement, then eased back a flap of muscle to expose what remained of Raust's forearm bones.

'I need to blunt these, or they'll cause more damage. Hand me a scalpel, my lord.'

The Lord Solar did as he was bid, and held aside the bloody flesh so Arnetz could work unimpeded. The silence hung heavy between them for a few minutes, broken only by the sound of the scalpel scraping against the rough bone as Arnetz waited for the Lord Solar to continue.

'I would understand any anger you felt towards me,' he said at last. 'After all, I led our forces into a resounding defeat today, and doubtless–'

'My lord, I am a soldier of Catachan,' Arnetz said, a chilled exhilaration playing across her skin as she interrupted the Lord Solar. 'I am given orders and I obey them. You are our commanding officer, and I will follow your orders, just as everyone else here will.'

'Thank you, Arnetz,' the Lord Solar said. 'But I fear at least a measure of your trust is misplaced.'

'How so, my lord?'

'Because I understand enough Attilan to know what they are saying,' he said, nodding over to where Nomak and Rugen were speaking with Belgutei. 'They want him to ask me to reconsider staying here. They think we'll have a better chance of survival if we make for the plains to the north.'

'Is that not a wise plan?' Arnetz asked as the Lord Solar adjusted his grip on Raust's arm, giving her better access to a spur of sharp bone. She would have struggled to do this alone, she realised, and the Lord Solar had proven himself to be a very capable assistant.

'We could survive on the plains for a time, but we would achieve nothing,' he said as she ran a blood-slicked finger over the newly blunted bone with an approving nod.

'The next part will be a little more difficult. Take a moment to rest your grip if you need to – I know it can be hard on your hands if you're not used to it,' Arnetz said, reaching for a threaded needle as the Lord Solar gave her a strange smile. 'So tell me, what will we achieve by staying here?'

'Victory,' he replied, as if it was obvious.

Arnetz opened a sachet of counterseptic powder, spread it liberally across the red, healthy flesh of Raust's cleaned wound, and began the long process of stitching it closed. She processed the Lord Solar's words as she worked, and only looked up when the last stitch was pulled taut, tied, and the thread cut with one last slice of the scalpel.

She could see the strength of the Lord Solar's conviction written across his features, but she could also see the weight of responsibility in the way he held himself, and the unimaginable fatigue behind his eyes.

Despite all she had seen over the last day, the fact they were so few and the orks so numerous, for a fleeting moment she found herself believing him.

'You can count on me, my lord,' Arnetz said.

'Thank you, corporal.' The Lord Solar nodded. 'That was good work and an honour to assist. If you ever decide to leave the front lines behind, I think that you'd be an asset to the chirurgical corps.'

Arnetz just laughed in response to that, the sudden levity fuelled by relief as much as the idea that she might live long enough to take up such a prestigious role. With a last check of Raust's vital signs, she pushed herself to her feet with a click of seized joints.

'I might take up that offer if we survive, but for now I think we deserve a drink.'

The cold water of the river stung Arnetz's skin as she washed Raust's blood from her hands and forearms, the gloves and soiled equipment piled up at her feet as she scrubbed. They were not so rich in resources that anything could be simply discarded, so she resolved to clean them in preparation for further use.

'Thank you for your help, my lord,' she said as the Lord Solar joined her at the riverside. 'You'd make a capable medicae's assistant with a little more training.'

'I'll be sure to add that to my list of accolades,' he said with a smile. 'It's one of the subjects we were taught in the scholam, topped up with some further study over the years. I've read about similar procedures in a number of treatises, some dating back as far as the second millennium.'

'You read about it in a book?' Arnetz asked in disbelief.

'Of course,' he said, and pulled the gloves from his hands. Arnetz let out a low whistle.

They were both augmetic: bare gun-grey metal facsimiles of skeletal hands, finely wrought but clearly crafted for utility rather than vanity. There was none of the gold chasing or filigree she'd seen on soft-worlder generals, nor the painted decorative plating of the Imperial nobility; they were the hands of a warrior, built to withstand the rigors of combat rather than the fine crystal neck of a courtier's wine flute.

'I'll admit that my research into this subject was driven by personal interest,' he said, slipping his white leather gloves back over his hands. With them on, it became impossible to see the telltale signs of augmentation; he became the vision of the Lord Solar once more, a paragon of human endeavour.

'Very fine work,' Arnetz said with an approving nod. 'I've seen similar amongst some of our officers, but I must admit that I expected something more decorative.'

'I needed hands that worked, not ones that looked good in picts,' the Lord Solar said with a laugh and plunged his head into the icy river, coming up a moment later in a spray of cold water.

She couldn't help but notice that he had chosen a point on the bank close to where the Attilans still spoke animatedly in hushed tones, their eyes flickering towards her and the Lord Solar as he wiped the water from his eyes. He made a show of cupping his hands to drink from the river, his eyes unfocused as he listened to the Rough Riders.

'I'm going to get some air,' he said after a moment. 'Send Belgutei to see me, then get some food and some rest, Arnetz. We will have further need of your skills before this is over.'

Still wiping the dripping water from his face as he walked away, the Lord Solar left Arnetz at the waterside and made for the dimming light of the cave mouth.

FOUR

Belgutei's leg throbbed with each hobbling step he took towards the cave mouth, the movement tugging at the staples holding his wounds closed. Nomak and Rugen's words still rang in his ears, begging and imploring him to speak to the Lord Solar and make him see sense – they were Attilans, bred to fight and die beneath an open sky, not the dead-eyed Krieg who fought in lightless trenches and tunnels dug beneath the earth.

As he had sent them away to feed and water the horses, he'd regretted not silencing their protests as soon as they had begun. Do-Song would have ended any talk of defying their orders at its outset. The old man could diffuse a raging conflict amongst his men the same way that water extinguished a lit candle, and yet still leave every man willing to die for him.

But Do-Song was dead. So were his honour guard, as far as Belgutei knew, alongside so many of the other Rough Riders who he had fought and bled alongside all his adult life. They would still be on the fields where they had fallen, their bodies unburied and unmourned, save for the few prayers he had made to the God-Emperor before his men had come to petition him.

A small part of him wanted to believe that there might be others who had forced their way free, escaping to the plains where he had made for the mountains, but his dim mood had smothered the embers of that vain hope. His comrades planetside were dead or, worse, captured. He could only pray that the Lord Solar hadn't committed the entire regiment to the initial landings – that there might be some who had never even made it to the surface.

That thought called forth the sickening image of burning troop landers streaking down through the clouds, the men, women, and horses within dying in flames...

He took a deep breath to calm himself, then stepped through the shadows of the cave's mouth and out into the slot canyon beyond, and made for the figure in gold.

The Lord Solar stood on a rocky outcrop at the centre of the river, surveying the canyon, his boots just clear of the foaming water. Thin shafts of light cut down from the summit high above, rays of pure luminescence that gave Leontus a golden radiance as they reflected from his armour.

'You wish to speak to me,' Belgutei said as he approached the Lord Solar.

'I do,' Leontus said, beckoning for Belgutei to join him. 'I need to know what the mood is amongst your men. I have spoken to each in turn, but I can't claim the kinship you have with them.'

'As well as can be expected,' Belgutei said, wincing as the staples pulled at his flesh. 'They... We survived today when so many did not. We will grieve for those lost when there is time, but they are still ready to fight at your command.'

'And you?'

'I can still ride. If an Attilan can ride, then they can fight.'

'I don't just need you to fight, I need you to lead,' Leontus said, his tone even. 'In order for that to happen I need you to think clearly.'

'With due respect, my lord, I am thinking clearly,' Belgutei said, swallowing the lie even as he realised what it was. He still felt strangely detached from himself, as if he was both within and outside of his mind at the same time, but couldn't communicate that to the Lord Solar.

'Indeed?' the Lord Solar said with a raised eyebrow. 'And the fact your men want you to petition me to ride north?'

Belgutei's teeth ground together as he realised what the Lord Solar must have overheard.

'You speak Attilan,' he said. It wasn't a question but a statement, one that was laced with accusation.

'Some. A people's language is a useful tool to help understand who they are.'

'And you understand us, my lord?' Belgutei asked, emphasising the last word.

'I understand that today's events are still fresh in all of our minds, but we shouldn't allow them to colour our decision-making,' the Lord Solar said. 'Nor should we give in to fear.'

'Fear? My lord, my men aren't giving in to fear – we would be safer on the move. A moving target is harder to hit, and out on the plains we have room to manoeuvre. Here we are trapped, like caged grox awaiting slaughter.'

'If we run now, we will always be a target, forever looking over our shoulders for the orks in their foul wagons and flying contraptions,' Leontus argued. 'Here we have shelter, a supply of water, and even food if there are fish in the lake or local wildlife to trap. Out on the plains, every moment would be laced with fear until we were found and slaughtered.'

'I am no coward. I do not fear death, and nor do my men,' Belgutei said defiantly. His leg throbbed as his body tensed, caught between his growing anger and deference to the Lord Solar. He stood arguing with a man who had fought the God-Emperor's enemies for over a century, wielding armies the same way Belgutei did his lance – with unerring, devastating precision. He had only ever seen the Lord Solar's noble features carved from marble or cast in hazy monochrome on a vid-screen, but no sculptor or pict had ever captured the sheer force of his gaze – the will that defended the Imperium's heart.

'You are no coward,' Leontus agreed after a few moments' pause, during which Belgutei's resolve cracked beneath the Lord Solar's attention. 'But you have lost your clarity of purpose, and I would help you find it again.'

'My lord?'

It was hardly the response he had expected, not from so senior an officer. He had anticipated a curt order to get himself in line, to follow where he was led, and to trust in his superior's judgement. At worst, he expected the Lord Solar to draw his famous pistol and end his life, putting him down the same way that commissars ended any dissension within the ranks. The Lord Solar sounded as if he almost understood the bleak mood that had gripped Belgutei since they had stopped running, not to mention the aimless anger and clouded judgement that dogged him even then.

'Why are we here, Belgutei?'

'On Fortuna Minor, my lord?'

'Yes. Why did I drag us all halfway across the segmentum to an ork-held agri world?'

'Because we are to liberate it from the xenos,' Belgutei said warily, repeating the scant information that he had been given in transit to Fortuna Minor, alongside the rest of the Attilan contingent.

'Yes, but why?'

It was a trick or a test, it had to be. Superior officers did not invite open thinking like this, not least from those beneath them.

'Because you ordered it, my lord. It is the will of the God-Emperor,' Belgutei said, and made the sign of the aquila over his heart as he hoped his words would mollify the Lord Solar.

'It is His will,' the Lord Solar said, 'but let me tell you why.'

He stepped down from the stone and led Belgutei from the water over to a patch of dry earth covered in rounded river stones, and took a seat on one of the boulders.

'Fortuna Minor itself is almost worthless – an agri world of open plains that supported a struggling livestock tradition. At least, before the orks came,' the Lord Solar explained, indicating for Belgutei to sit beside him. 'It became significant when the growing Waaagh! of Warboss Iron Tooth – or "Irontoof", to use the ork parlance – chose to take its meagre resources to fuel his campaign.'

'So we came to Fortuna Minor to liberate it?' Belgutei asked.

'In part. It is only a small section of a larger tapestry,' Leontus said. He scooped up a trio of smooth river stones and set them out in a shallow curve on the rock beside Belgutei. 'The centre is the Fortuna System, and Waaagh! Iron Tooth. To the galactic west is the Ullanax System, which lies in the path of Waaagh! Blue Tongue, and the Tegron System to the east is under attack by Waaagh! Dead Eye. Each is a minor threat to the security of the Segmentum Solar alone, but were their forces to combine…'

The Lord Solar raised an eyebrow, allowing Belgutei's mind to finish his sentence for him.

'I understand,' Belgutei said, leaving the threat unspoken.

'If we stop Waaagh! Iron Tooth on Fortuna Minor, it increases the chances that the two other Waaagh!s will pass one another like ships in the night,' the Lord Solar said, and kicked away the centre stone to emphasise his point. 'Their forces never combine and can be dealt with individually.'

'A bold strategy, my lord,' Belgutei said.

'Bold, but backed up by the Collegiate Astrolex. They studied the tarot a thousand times, reading fates and interrogating the weft of destiny's shadow in the warp. In every foretelling, our victory here ensured the orks' paths would never cross.'

Belgutei shuddered involuntarily as the Lord Solar mentioned the Collegiate Astrolex, his personal coterie of seers, psychics and tarot readers – witches all, in Belgutei's opinion.

'They did not foresee what happened today?'

'They did not,' Leontus said with a bitter grimace, 'and neither did I. But we are in a better position than you might realise.'

'How so, my lord?' Belgutei asked.

'Because Warboss Iron Tooth was killed nine days ago aboard his ship, alongside the majority of his forces in orbit.'

Belgutei found himself staring as his understanding of the warzone they were trapped in shifted.

'But if their warboss is already dead...'

'Then the lieutenants will fight for dominance amongst themselves, leaving them scattered and vulnerable. It is behaviour we have observed before, and thought we could capitalise on here.'

Belgutei thought back to the landing fields, to the screaming hordes of orks that had apparently been waiting for them as their landers crashed down in flames, pursued by xenos aircraft even as they burned. He remembered fighting through a ring of bare-skinned savages and the lines of black-armoured Goffs beyond them, two distinct forces that battled on despite the attentions of the Speed Freeks.

'We were dropped into the middle of a battle,' Belgutei said as he realised how doomed they had been.

'One that should have been cleared by lance and orbital bombardment before a single trooper set foot on Fortuna Minor,' Leontus agreed, his body language changing subtly as his expression darkened. 'The landings and the bombardment should have begun simultaneously, one clearing the ground for the other. As I was part of the first landing wave, I was on my lander when I received word from orbit – the orbital strikes had to be abandoned to protect the troop ships from an incoming force. I enacted one of my contingency plans should this exact eventuality occur – the fleet are to stage a fighting withdrawal to the edge of the system and regroup before attacking again.'

'You ordered them to retreat rather than fight to the death,' Belgutei said, though his own thoughts were far darker in tone. The Lord Solar had ordered the fleet to withdraw and to leave every soldier on Fortuna Minor to die, including himself. They were alone on this world, with no prospect of rescue in the foreseeable future.

'I abandoned a failing strategy in favour of one that had a higher probability of success,' the Lord Solar said. 'The fleet will return.'

'That could take weeks, my lord.'

Leontus nodded. 'If not months. I don't know what forces came upon them in orbit, but they must not have been insignificant. What matters is that we are ready to meet them when they do return.'

A black thought crossed Belgutei's mind, though he didn't

give voice to it – what if the fleet hadn't been driven off, but destroyed? What if they were truly alone on Fortuna Minor?

'You have a plan then?' he asked instead.

'Several. But they all end with us taking the space port back from the orks.'

'So we can get off-world and back to the fleet,' Belgutei said, a flicker of something like hope stirring in his gut.

He became aware of the Lord Solar watching him, his dark eyes inscrutable in the dim light as Belgutei considered the different paths ahead of him.

They could ride north and likely die to the mobs of Speed Freeks scouring the continent. If the Lord Solar refused to join them, they could leave him here, where orks hunting through the hillsides would eventually find him. That would mean death on the plains too, or a summary execution by firing squad if they were lucky enough to survive until the fleet's return. Or they could remain, under the direct command of a man who was said to be the tactical equal of Saint Macharius himself, and fight their way free of the xenos…

There was only one decision that called to him.

'I am with you, my lord.'

'Good. Very good,' the Lord Solar said, and he offered his hand to Belgutei.

Belgutei wiped his palm on his coat before accepting the handshake, though the rough material did little to clean the dirt, dust, sweat, and ork blood that had congealed on his skin. Leontus took it all the same, and shook it in a surprisingly strong grip. Belgutei pushed aside the thought of what he would have to tell Nomak, Rugen and Csaba, who had all made their opinions clear.

'We will ride out at first light to see what we are up against,' the Lord Solar said. He pushed himself to his feet, his eyes drawn to the dark skies just visible through the canyon's upper reaches. Streaks of white slashed across the darkness visible between the canyon's high walls, falling stars that had once been ships, Belgutei thought, though it was impossible to tell if they were of human or xenos origin.

'It doesn't seem fair, taking on a world with four Attilans, a Catachan medicae, and a one-armed Krieg,' he said with a sad smile. The Lord Solar looked at him like a statue carved of cold marble, every inch the inspiring leader that the artists and sculptors made him out to be.

'And one Lord Solar.'

'Well? What did he say?' Nomak asked as Belgutei returned, limping over to where Gori's saddle had been laid on the cold stone floor. The horse was hitched with the others against the cavern wall, the animals' faces enclosed within their feed bags.

'We stay,' Belgutei said as he pulled out Do-Song's bedroll and set it out by his saddle; his own was likely lost wherever Nomi had escaped to, and he didn't think Do-Song would much care in any case.

'And you agreed?' Nomak said.

'It's not for me to agree or disagree. He's the Lord Solar.'

'And that's enough for you?'

'Is it not for you?' Belgutei asked with a sigh. For a few blessed moments, the only sound was the babbling of rushing water and the occasional clatter of hooves as the horses rearranged themselves, and Belgutei almost had time to relax.

'Belgutei is right. He is the Lord Solar, we should listen–' Csaba began, but Nomak's laughter cut across him.

'Ha! And what would you know about it? You've barely broken your twentieth lance.'

'I am a rider,' Csaba hissed. 'Just as much as you are.'

'I think,' Rugen said, his deep, calm voice lent a slight sibilance by his scarred lips, 'that whatever we do, it must be together. Attilans are strongest as a group – alone we are just prey.'

All that Belgutei wanted was to close his eyes and escape into his dreams, to leave the pains and fears of the waking world behind and find some measure of peace in the darkness, but it would have to wait.

'We could run, and if we do we will never stop,' Belgutei said. 'Or we could remain here with the Lord Solar, and find a way off-world.'

'The Lord Solar has a plan?' Csaba asked. There was hope in the young man's eyes then, a brightness that Belgutei struggled to feel himself.

'He does. But he needs us all to see it done.'

He looked from Rugen to Csaba, confident that he had won them around at least. Nomak was harder to read, his shadowed features inscrutable in the darkness.

'Tomorrow is another day. Let us see what it brings,' Nomak said, and rolled over to face away from the other Attilans.

'Csaba, you take first watch,' Belgutei ordered, his eyes lingering on his second-in-command.

He lay back against Gori's saddle and tried to find the peace he yearned for as Csaba made for the cave's mouth, but it slipped through his fingers like sand. Every time he closed his eyes, all he saw was an old friend reaching down to him from the saddle, before whirring blades tore him in two.

FIVE

Whilst the others slept, Leontus prayed.

He'd set the Radiant Helm on the folded cloth of his cloak alongside his pistol, Sol's Righteous Gaze, and his power sword, Conquest, in the deep recesses of the upper level of the cavern.

He prayed first for those who had died on the landing fields, that their souls might fly quickly across the tempestuous heavens and find true peace at the God-Emperor's side. He thanked Him for His mercy in allowing so many into His golden radiance, and for granting them their final rest.

Then he prayed for the men and women of the fleet, that they fight their way clear of the ork menace and return swiftly to Fortuna Minor to continue the righteous cleansing that was vital to the Segmentum Solar's continued security.

Then he prayed to the saint that he had taken as his own, to guide him through the infinite perils that faced humanity.

'Sainted Macharius, I beg your guidance,' Leontus whispered to the Radiant Helm, as if it were an improvised shrine. There was no sudden revelation nor holy sign; his faith was something more intimate and far more subtle than such overt miracles. He did not rely on holy lightning to strike down his foes, but on sound tactical planning and the judicious application of artillery. The coming days would show if the saint had heard his plea.

His final prayer was more personal, and tinged with regret.

'God-Emperor. As your humble servant I beg you to bestow your grace on Tempestor Ignaci Udon, Sergeant Tobin Sherudev, and troopers Hautin and Longinus, for their service in your name, and their sacrifice that I might live.'

The last moments aboard his Aquila lander flashed before his eyes. Smoke. Blood. Fire. Hard rounds stitching a line of sparks and searing metal through the compartment, before an ork missile bit through the reinforced bulkheads like an ocean predator tearing flesh from its prey. Shouting orders to Fleetmaster Emmin over the screeching vox when Ignaci tackled him from the holo-table, saving him from the barking gunfire that blew the table apart. Being pushed into the saviour pod that had been retrofitted for this exact purpose as fire consumed the shuttle, and then falling...

He let out a long, slow, controlled breath and tried to visualise the tension leaving his body, just as his personal physicians had once taught him, and applied cold logic to the challenges ahead as he looked out across the sleeping forms on the cavern floor below.

Belgutei's mind was still adrift on a melancholic sea; Leontus had lit the torch on a distant shore, but it would be up to the Attilan to navigate his own path through the turbulent waters of fatalism. It hadn't felt good to lie to the Attilan about his reasons for needing to take the space port, even if it had just been a lie of omission, but it had been necessary. He had no intention of leaving Fortuna Minor, but Belgutei and his men were Leontus' greatest resource; if the Attilan could find his way clear of his spiritual ennui then they would be a swift hammer, capable of bringing even the mightiest of foes to their knees.

Lying had never come naturally to him, but it was a skill he had been forced to hone in order to survive courtly life in the Imperial Palace, where a man as powerful as the Lord Solar had to watch his allies as vigilantly as his enemies. He had learned to lace a lie with enough truth to make it believable, weaving facts through the fiction to create a rich tapestry where one thread couldn't be separated from another. In the more humble surroundings of Fortuna Minor, the deceit left a sour taste on his tongue.

Belgutei's men appeared to have taken their sergeant's decision as well as could be hoped for, but the next day would see how many remained by their sergeant's side. It wouldn't be unheard of or unexpected for at least one to desert their post, but Leontus prayed that his words to the Attilan might be enough for them to be swayed.

Arnetz stirred as Csaba returned from his turn on watch, barely visible to Leontus from her shadowed niche above Raust's prone form. Like most of the people of her world, her brash exterior concealed hidden depths and an unbending spirit, adding dimensions to the muscle-bound caricatures some believed Catachans to be. She saw and understood more than others might perceive, which made her a useful resource beyond her value as a skilled medicae.

What he needed now was to understand the scale of the enemy they faced: their numbers, their disposition and their locations. In doing so, he might also discover the fate of any Imperial survivors, be they in captivity or in hiding just as he was, and the opportunities that they might present.

At dawn, he would head out with some of Belgutei's riders to scout the surrounding area and gather the information he needed.

Then he could plan his war.

Leontus led the scouting party out before dawn, following the path of the river through the canyon under the grey light of a new day on Fortuna Minor. The last vestiges of night fled to the deepest corners of the canyon to await their turn to dominate the land once more.

Leontus had ordered that the scout party forgo the horses' barding and armour, preferring speed over battlefield durability; if they were caught by orks in any great numbers, there would be little chance of fighting their way clear. Escape would be the better option. It also helped that Arnetz had volunteered to remain behind, ostensibly to guard the cavern and to watch over Raust, but also because she would only slow them down as they scouted the surroundings. Csaba had been more reluctant to stay, but the young Attilan had done as he was ordered.

'You know what we need,' Leontus said as he halted the riders, looking out over a bank of thick mist that drifted over the water's surface and out across the plateau. 'Don't engage. Don't get caught. Don't return to the cavern before dark.'

Nomak and Rugen made noises of assent and rode away into the mist together; they knew their role and what was expected of them. On the face of it, they were to scout the eastern bank of the lake and mark any notable settlements or structures on the plains below, whilst Leontus did the same to the west with Belgutei. In truth, it was a test, and one that Leontus hoped they wouldn't fail.

He rode to the edge of the plateau with Belgutei, where the cold wind from the mountain had begun to clear the morning mist into a whirling haze. It rolled over the contours of the hills down towards the plains, filling the crevasses and dried river cuts as if they weren't there, and settled in the shadowed contours of the foothills miles below. Leontus' eyes flicked to the brightening sky, the dull grey crystallising into a cloudless blue that would have matched the colour of his uniform had it not been caked in dust and flecks of mud.

'I keep looking for their airborne threats too, my lord,' Belgutei said.

'We'd hear them before we saw them, but we can't be too careful,' Leontus said. 'There – that promontory will make a good vantage point.'

They dismounted near a limestone outcrop and led their horses towards a low rise overlooking the lake to the east and the foothills to the west. Beyond the misted green of undulating ridges lay the sun-scarred grasslands of the plains, an almost featureless expanse that held back the endless horizon.

Belgutei handed him a pair of ornate antique magnoculars from his saddlebags, and Leontus took a moment to admire the hand-beaten brass casing and carefully maintained lenses. They were no substitute for a fleet's auspex arrays, nor the corps of logisticians and analysts he usually relied upon, but they would have to be enough.

'There's a camp due west,' Leontus said after a moment's scanning of the vista, the magnoculars auto-focusing on an earth-walled encampment that was nothing more than a blemish on the horizon with his naked eyes. Tiny figures were rendered into dark blurs by the distance, but it was clear to see that the orks were riding huge bipedal beasts that snapped and bit at one another.

He looked away and offered the magnoculars to Belgutei. 'Five miles distant at least.'

The Attilan took them and zeroed in on the camp, his teeth grinding as he looked upon his enemy once more. 'Beast Snaggas.'

'That was my assumption,' Leontus said, and took back the magnoculars.

'We didn't fight any Beast Snaggas on the landing fields,' Belgutei muttered.

'Perhaps they were elsewhere on the battlefield,' Leontus said. 'Or else they weren't there at all.'

He scanned south of the Beast Snaggas camp, noting how quickly the mists were burned away by the rising sun. It was a fleeting advantage but a usable one, especially for a force that couldn't rely on weight of numbers, and so he made a mental note of it.

'There's a structure to the south-west – is that the space port?' Belgutei asked. 'There, over the sharp stone peak, do you see it?'

'It's the space port,' Leontus said as he focused on the distant tower, which reached high into the sky like a taloned finger topped with a cracked gem that glimmered in the morning sun. The dull grey of the tower's body was rent and gapped by long-quenched fires, revealing the mesh of reinforcement bars running through the plascrete shell and the warped structures within. But the hive of activity at the tower's base was what caught his eye: a ring of blackened metal was taking shape around the space port's scattered hangars, warehouses and storage sheds, and even the tower itself. Orks swarmed through the structures in streams of green flesh as they attended to their barbaric whims, working on ramshackle machines daubed in red paint or brawling over scavenged materiel. The choicest pieces were dragged towards a hangar nestled at the base of the tower, rendered squat by distance but which must have been two hundred feet tall at its zenith.

'That looks more organised than I would like,' Leontus muttered, and Belgutei made a noise of assent.

'Could it be that the orks have rallied around a new leader?' the Attilan asked.

'It should have taken them longer than this for one of the lieutenants to take full control,' Leontus said.

He ran through the possibilities in his mind, searching the libraries of information he'd read and written on the unpredictability of the orks. It was unlikely, but not inconceivable.

'The ork that Arnetz killed on the landing field, with Raust,' Belgutei said, as if suddenly realising something. 'It was the largest xenos on that field by a margin. Perhaps–'

'I had teams monitoring their communication channels on the approach to Fortuna Minor and there was no intelligence that they had a new warboss, just a reference to the "Head Nobz",' Leontus said. 'It's most likely that one of the lieutenants has taken the space port and is fortifying it against attack by Imperial forces… And its competitors.'

'So there's at least two of them fighting for leadership.'

'Maybe. We've found out as much as we're going to from here, we should head south.'

He took Belgutei's silence as agreement and turned to the south, towards the plumes of roiling black smoke that had been dancing at the corners of their eyes since light had washed the night from Fortuna Minor. The landing fields would have to be surveyed in order to get a complete picture of their surroundings, but Leontus was as reluctant as Belgutei to see it again with his own eyes.

* * *

He didn't need the magnoculars to see the bloody wound on Fortuna Minor's surface. Crumpled hulks of fallen landers still burned, their smoke combining into a sky-blackening tumble of lightless smoke that left the battlefield in the shade. The bodies of humans lay intertwined with innumerable orks on the gore-stained ground, a dark morass of death that Leontus knew his eyes would never be able to unsee.

'God-Emperor protect them,' Belgutei said, and turned away.

But Leontus kept looking, scorching every aspect of the sight into his brain like a brand marking cattle. The Imperium would raise no monuments to the dead below him; the galaxy would not mourn, nor would the Administratum so much as blink at the numbers of the lost.

Leontus would remember them.

'Have you seen enough, my lord?'

Belgutei wasn't looking down at the battlefield but at him, Leontus realised. He hoped that his emotions hadn't been clearly written on his features. Belgutei needed the Lord Solar to be an inviolable sentinel against the darkness, not a grief-stricken old man who had led hundreds to their deaths on a fallen world.

Leontus squared his jaw and held out his hand for the magnoculars. Belgutei passed them over without another word and turned to the battlefield, his head bowed in prayer.

The sight was no better with the magnoculars' zoom, though he was able to read the ebb and flow of the battle that had taken place: the central ring of black-armoured Goff orks who had been assailed from all sides by their savage brethren, before the Imperial forces' disastrous arrival; the furious defences on the thresholds of burning landers; a beachhead cut through the ork lines to a downed dakkajet and then on to a Krieg gunline. He could even make out the path of the Attilan charge that had burst free from the melee, reading a churned trail of hoof-marked earth that led back to the battle and was lost beneath dead horses and fallen orks.

His eye was drawn to other tracks in the earth, where heavy vehicles and iron-shod boots had come and gone after the battle was done. Diminutive figures were still visible on the field, dragging sacks and sleds filled with the battle's detritus.

'Such a place needs a name to honour those who died there,' Belgutei said, pulling Leontus from his study of the battle-field and the trails that led away from it.

'Bruke.'

'My lord?'

'The libraries of Terra speak of an ancient warrior, Eolbert of Bruke, who ruled long before mankind looked to the stars. His people were enslaved, and he waged war to free them.'

'A noble endeavour.'

Leontus nodded. 'It was, but Bruke tasted defeat many times before he finally usurped the tyrant that ruled his lands. After one such defeat he found himself in a cave by the sea, and contemplated fleeing and leaving the war behind. It was there that he saw a spider building its web, only for the sea's swell to destroy what it had built, again and again, until it at last found a way to complete its work.'

'I have never liked spiders,' Belgutei said.

'It's not about spiders, but about holding your course no matter what obstacles you find in your way,' Leontus replied. 'Once he became king, Bruke told the story of the spider's perseverance and how it had given him the strength to continue. Of course, like most Terran legends the story is likely embellished – if it ever happened at all – but the message still stands.'

Belgutei was quiet for a while, his features unreadable.

At last, he said, 'We will persevere, my lord. For those that died at Bruke.'

'We will, together,' Leontus told him, and looked over to the east, where a growing cloud of dust was forming on the plateau.

'It's Nomak,' Belgutei said.

The young Attilan corporal rode at pace across the plateau with Rugen following in his wake, their horses kicking up a cloud of dust as they made for the Lord Solar at speed. Leontus was more pleased to see them than he could let on – they had passed his test by returning, and not abandoning the others to a slim chance of escape across the plains.

'Slow down, damn you! Can't you see the dust?' Belgutei roared as they came within earshot.

'These blunt-minded beasts can't see us up here,' Nomak said with a grin. 'But you will want to see what we have found.'

'There are humans inside,' Belgutei breathed, the borrowed magnoculars shaking in his hands as he lowered them from his disbelieving eyes.

Nomak had been giddy as they rode to the eastern edge of the plateau, his mouth running almost as fast as his horse as he urged the other riders to greater speed. *There are two camps within spitting distance of one another – one seems to be a Speed Freeks enclave, filled with their rickety vehicles, machine parts and fuel containers,'* he had said over his shoulder. *'The other… You won't believe this, either of you, but there are people in there!'*

'Prisoners of the Waaagh!,' Leontus said, lowering Do-Song's ornate magnoculars as his brows furrowed. 'Deathskulls in the southern camp, Speed Freeks in the northern camp.'

They knelt on the edge of a steep escarpment carpeted by

thick grasses and low shrubs, its lower reaches scarred by a landslide that had gouged the slope's surface. Despite Nomak's assurance that they wouldn't be spotted so far from the orks below, Leontus had insisted upon caution.

Belgutei raised the magnoculars again, hoping that his eyes hadn't given way to the blind hope in his heart. They were still there: slight, human frames clearly visible over the right-hand camp's walls, distinct from the stooping, heavy-shouldered orks that bustled around the ramshackle structures. Most of the prisoners appeared to be on their feet and moving, which was an encouraging sign.

'I told you there were survivors,' Nomak said, barely able to contain his own excitement. 'We could–'

'What else have you seen, other than these two camps?' the Lord Solar asked.

'There is a river that leads off to the south, passing just west of the camps, which looks to be fed from the lake,' Nomak said. He pointed due west of the twin camps to a shimmering ribbon that wound across the terrain to the south. 'The source must be behind the hills below, but the orks seem to be able to cross it at will.'

'Which suggests that it is fordable or that there is a bridge,' Leontus mused. 'Anything else?'

'There is a downed ship to the north-east, though I can't tell if it's one of ours or theirs, my lord.'

'A problem for another day,' Leontus said.

Belgutei listened to their exchange in his periphery, but found that he couldn't focus on their words. There were men and women in the camp below – Astra Militarum soldiers who had survived the landing field massacre too. He couldn't leave them there to rot with the xenos, penned in like cattle awaiting slaughter.

Then a lone figure stepped out of the Deathskulls camp, its face and mismatched armour daubed in blue paint, and began to scream something at the Speed Freeks camp. Belgutei couldn't hear whatever it was saying, but it had an almost immediate effect on the orks in the other encampment. An ork in what appeared to be a butchered Imperial Navy pilot's jacket emerged from between one of the many massive gaps in the camp's walls, the material likely scavenged to build their ramshackle vehicles. It took a few steps forward and started screaming in response to the Deathskull, and crowds began to form behind each of them.

'Something's happening,' Belgutei said, motioning for the others' attention.

With frightening speed, both groups suddenly surged forward as the orks charged at one another across the few hundred yards between them, their war cries carrying over the foothills to where Belgutei knelt. His body tingled with sudden adrenaline, and he had the urge to have his sword in his hand.

'They're fighting each other?' Nomak said in surprise from behind his own magnoculars.

Both camps had all but emptied, their occupants rushing out through their gates with such speed that they were torn from their hinges, the massive metal plates crushing any orks too slow to get out of the way. The others didn't slow, but ran ahead to meet their foes in a whirling melee of fists and teeth.

'Did you see what instigated it?' the Lord Solar asked, Do-Song's magnoculars pressed hard against his eyes. He let in a sharp intake of breath as if he'd spotted something in the camp that Belgutei and the others hadn't, but didn't explain what.

'One came out and started screaming something, though I have no idea what it was saying.'

The Lord Solar ran his tongue over his teeth again as he considered something, looking from Belgutei to the others as if measuring them up.

'We could ride down now whilst they're fighting, rescue some of the prisoners?' Nomak suggested, but the Lord Solar shook his head.

'We wouldn't get there in time. We would need to be ready to strike the moment the orks commit to fighting one another,' he said. 'Belgutei, which is your fastest horse?' he asked.

'Gori, by a long way,' Belgutei replied. 'Why? What are you thinking, my lord?'

'That we have an opportunity to increase our odds of success,' the Lord Solar said, and began to unclasp his cloak.

'This is insane.'

'I know,' Belgutei said.

'He's going to get us all killed.'

Belgutei nodded. 'Most likely.' Nashi whickered beside him and made to stand, but he calmed her with a low, soothing voice.

'Are you listening to me, Belgutei?' Nomak asked.

'No,' Belgutei said, keeping the smile from his face.

He felt alive again, back in the moment, with his men by his side and a target in front of him. The Lord Solar's plan was an audacious one, but the man was famous for achieving what other men said could not be done.

Belgutei, Rugen, and Nomak were hidden on the riverbank south of the Deathskulls camp, crouched next to their horses in the tall reeds that lined both sides of the winding river. The horses were lying in the sodden mud next to their riders, a feat that required years of training for Attilan warhorses to learn. It had taken over an hour to get into position without being seen by the orks, to find the source of the river, and to swim their horses downstream and under the ramshackle bridge that the xenos had constructed over its waters.

Belgutei kept his eyes on the camp's totem, just visible above the thick reeds – a glowering blue ork skull fashioned from hammered metal and decorated with actual skulls that looked uncomfortably human.

'Do you see him?' Belgutei asked Rugen, who was higher on the riverbank than the others.

'I do not see him,' the older Attilan replied.

The Lord Solar had taken a different route down the mountain, riding due east of the plateau towards the open ground north of the two ork camps, and it was possible that he wasn't even in position yet.

'The orks are going back to their camps,' Rugen hissed, waving Belgutei up the slope to look.

Belgutei passed Nashi's reins to Nomak and crawled through the reeds hand over hand until he was at Rugen's side. He took the offered magnoculars and saw orks limping back to the camp from their little battle. Most seemed battered and bruised but otherwise elated, but there were many prone forms left on the ground in both sides' colours.

'Remember, we need to hit the rear of the camp as soon as he rides through. If we can see him, that is,' Belgutei muttered, scanning the hazy horizon for any sign of the Lord Solar, until his eyes settled on a growing cloud of dust.

'That's him,' Rugen said with a gap-toothed smile.

'Prepare the lances and get ready to move.'

SIX

Gori's stride was solid, her rhythm perfectly even as she galloped across the plains. If the weight of Leontus' cloak bothered her as it trailed behind, the horse gave no sign, but barrelled forward at punishing speed. The Lord Solar rode high in the saddle, his body moving in time with Gori's thunderous pace, his eyes fixed on the ork camp ahead.

In his study of orks, drawn from both first-hand experience and second-hand accounts, he had identified a multitude of ways that they left themselves tactically exposed at almost every level. Their many weaknesses were overcome in the main by sheer ferocity and weight of numbers, with little to no plan other than to smash what lay in front of them; that suited Leontus, as it meant that the orks were often far too busy watching the most obvious target to notice what approached them from behind.

The red-daubed walls seemed to grow as he approached,

starting as a scarlet line on the horizon and becoming a gap-toothed maw of looming metal plates the colour of blood. His heart hammered beneath his dust-grimed breastplate, his rational mind screaming at him to turn back before he was seen and cut down, that the orks wouldn't take the bait and his plan was doomed to fail.

Leontus drew in a short, sharp breath, tasting the dust on the air mingled with Gori's musty sweat, and rode through one of the many wide gaps in the Speed Freeks encampment walls and into a crowd of shocked-looking orks.

Their camp was less of a fortified position than an untidy workshop with a few patches of wall still standing, the welded plates having been scavenged for their insane creations. The dust billowed through the camp in Leontus' wake, obscuring him for a moment as it settled on the xenos that stared at him in open-mouthed surprise.

Sol's Righteous Gaze blazed with incandescent rage, blasting a scorched hole through the nearest ork and the pile of tools behind it; a second shot slagged the cockpit of a three-wheeled buggy, pilot and metal alike, and the third ignited a bowser of promethium in a column of searing heat.

That was enough to shake the xenos out of their surprise and back to their primary state of being.

Gori reared up as they let out their bellowing war cries. The orks grabbed whatever tools were nearest as they charged towards the intruder, falling over one another as they scrambled to land the first blow. Leontus was already moving, whipping Gori into motion as the first of the xenos flung themselves into the air where he had been only heartbeats before. He launched Gori towards an open space in the gapped walls, firing his pistol at any ork that got too close, until he was free of the press and galloping breathlessly towards the Deathskulls camp. The explosive roar of engines starting behind him told him that the first step of the plan had been a success; all that remained was the second half.

He could see that the commotion hadn't yet drawn the attention of the Deathskulls – either they didn't care that their erstwhile kin were under attack, or they were simply used to the noise. It was that short-sightedness that Leontus was going to exploit.

A hard round slapped into the ground ahead of him, and he smiled, hearing the roar of pursuing engines from the Speed Freeks camp. He turned in the saddle to see their dust cloud rising higher than his own, obscuring everything behind them. Bullets sprayed from the weapons of drivers and gunners alike, fizzing past Leontus like angry insects on a faraway death world.

'Go, Gori! Move!' Leontus shouted, whipping the reins in an attempt to urge a little more pace from his mount. The horse found yet more speed and lurched forward, panting hard as she closed the distance between Leontus and the Deathskulls camp; its gates were mercifully still open, their under-engineered hinges sagging beneath the weight of the heavy plated doors.

'Don't let me down, Belgutei,' Leontus hissed, his words lost to the wind and the screaming of engines that sounded close enough for him to touch.

Ahead, the orks in the Deathskulls camp were finally taking notice of the Speed Freeks' charge, running to grab weapons and prepare for the attackers racing towards them. Leontus only needed them to hold their fire a little longer, just a few seconds…

With a tug on a worn leather cord, he released the ropes tying the cloak to his saddle and pulled hard on Gori's reins. The heavy material flopped to the earth in a dust-encrusted pile, the rocks tied to the ragged hem dragging it down as Leontus broke to the right and away from the path of the oncoming Speed Freeks under the cover of his own dust trail.

The camp's walls whipped past in a blur of badly painted metal, hard rounds hissing around him as the Deathskulls tried their luck with their brutal firearms. They quickly lost interest as he galloped out of their sight and around the side of the camp, finding far more enticing targets in the oncoming vehicles of their rivals.

Gori's breathing was laboured, her flanks slick with a mix of sweat and dust as she raced on. Leontus turned away from the grisly trophies hanging from the camp walls – the skeletal and half-rotted remains of humans and orks swinging from barbed hooks – though whether they were meant as a warning to outsiders or grim decoration, he couldn't say. What did become clear was that several of the disembodied limbs were far fresher than the others, the blood still glistening in browning trails where it stained the walls beneath.

A titanic impact set the grim trophies to dancing on their hooks as the Speed Freeks' charge slammed into the Deathskulls camp behind him. He smiled at that, clearing the walls in time to see Belgutei, Nomak, and Rugen charging towards him in the distance.

Without slowing Gori's gallop, Leontus steered the horse in a wide arc to bring himself to the back of the charging Attilans, the sounds of ork combat lost between the distance and the hammering of his mount's hooves.

'Strike at the wall and follow me through!' Leontus shouted as Gori brought him alongside the lance-carrying Attilans. Only then did he slow the horse's pace, putting a little protective distance between himself and Belgutei's riders; he would need it for what came next.

As one, Belgutei, Nomak, and Rugen turned from their charge at the very last second, wrenching their steeds away from a headlong gallop into the wall's riveted and welded metal plates, and used the last of their momentum to launch their explosive-tipped lances like thrown spears.

The wall disappeared in a sudden shockwave of light and heat, the melta charges chewing through plate steel and blue-daubed flakboard like a las-bolt through unprotected flesh. Dust billowed from the detonation in a choking cloud, carpeting the escaping Attilans as they brought their horses around for a second charge, but not so thick that Leontus couldn't see the new path into the camp.

'Go, Gori!' Leontus cried, holstering Sol's Righteous Gaze to grip the reins with both hands.

The horse responded as if they had been bonded for a lifetime, surging forward into the thinning dust cloud and the camp beyond.

Dazed orks bounced from Gori's flanks as they charged through a throng of the xenos, heading straight for the cages. Leontus needed to get as many prisoners out as possible before the battling Speed Freeks and Deathskulls realised that their fight was an engineered distraction and turned on the humans. He passed improvised cookhouses and rough bedding in a blur of muted colours, piles of scavenged flak armour and meat that still wore Astra Militarum uniforms. Those that still lived shouted to him as he approached, reaching for him through the rusting bars of their cages as they recognised the figure in blue and gold.

In a flash of rough-cast iron, accompanied by the scream of a wounded horse, the saddle was wrenched down with violent force. Leontus didn't have time to do anything but curl his arms over his head as he was thrown through the air.

Colours flashed before his eyes as the sky, earth, and rows of cages tumbled around him until the hard-packed ground met him with bruising force.

He let out an air-starved grunt of pain and anger as the last of his momentum rolled him to his feet, just in time to side-step the burly ork's first swing of its brutal maul. Two more orks emerged from the cages behind it, the furthest creature's axe buried in Gori's skull.

The burly ork was large and fast, relying on aggression and strength to heft its heavy weapon two-handed, each blow powerful enough to dent the armour of a Leman Russ but slow and obvious enough for him to dodge. How had his forces been undone by such inefficient beasts?

Sol's Righteous Gaze slipped into his hand like the hand-shake of an old friend, blasting away the ork's legs as Conquest left its scabbard. Motes of blue light flickered in its wake as he drew and slashed with a single, precise movement; the ork fell into the path of the swinging blade, and its head rolled clear of its hunched shoulders in a splash of black ichor. The second ork was already charging before its dead comrade had stopped twitching, its crude pistol spitting bullets as it leaped at the Lord Solar with a bestial roar.

Fingers of golden lightning flickered around Leontus as his refractor field deflected the few rounds that were on target, and he raised Sol's Righteous Gaze as his opponent's weapon clicked empty. The archeotech pistol felt hot in his hand, and he pulled the trigger, blasting the ork's torso into wet strings of bloody viscera as the captured humans cheered him on.

The final ork stepped over the ruined meat of Gori's skull, its beady red eyes taking in the little human in blue and gold that had killed two of its kind in only a few moments. Leon-tus lifted Conquest in a challenge that even the dull mind of an ork couldn't misunderstand, and holstered his pistol. Sol's Righteous Gaze needed time to cool before he used it again, so it would just be him against the ork – Lord Solar against xenos, ancient relic against blood-smeared iron.

That was the moment that Belgutei, Nomak, and Rugen rode through the hole blasted by their melta-tipped lances, their lasguns already flaring to punch the creature off Gori's corpse and into the dirt.

'They took the bait!' Belgutei said as he dragged on Nashi's reins.

'They did. Get the cages open,' Leontus said, his eyes on the furious melee that roiled like boiling oil at the camp's gates, spitting severed limbs and broken orks with each passing second. It had been a desperate gamble to draw the xenos away from their captives by using the Speed Freeks as bait; he'd known that it would work if he executed the plan properly, but now that the orks were distracted, they had to move fast to liberate as many soldiers as possible before the creatures realised what was happening behind them.

He slashed at the heavy locks with Conquest, the sword's power field crackling as it sliced deep gouges in the rough iron. Belgutei and his riders did the same, sliding from their saddles to move between the cages and shoot them open with their lasguns, all encouraged by desperate-eyed Astra Militarum soldiers.

'Move, run towards the river!' Leontus shouted as Conquest turned another lock to melted slag. He wrenched the cage's door open and pulled a soldier aside, noting the sergeant's stripes stitched onto his sleeve. 'What's your name, soldier?'

'Andersson, Lord Solar!' the man said, his violet eyes signifying his Cadian origins better than the standard-issue uniform he wore.

'Get your men to the river, Andersson – keep them together!'

Andersson nodded and turned back to the other occupants of his cage, barking orders for them to move and pointing the way out of the camp as Leontus moved on. Escaping troopers swarmed past him away from the embattled orks, some muttering their thanks as they ran whilst others supported wounded or weakened comrades.

Leontus looked about for the cage that he had seen from the plateau, one that he couldn't leave the camp without unlocking...

'Gori.'

Belgutei had stopped, his sword hanging loose in his hand as he approached his fallen mount.

'I'm sorry, Belgutei. I couldn't have done it without her,' Leontus said, sidestepping the Attilan to slash at the door to a cage containing three Catachans.

'May you find Do-Song and ride together at the God-Emperor's side,' Belgutei said, placing a hand on the horse's neck. When he looked up his expression was cold, his sword held tightly in his grip once more.

'Orks turning!' Nomak shouted, loosing a volley of shots into a pair of xenos who had realised that something was going on towards the rear of the encampment. The first fell, half of its skull vaporised by las-fire, but the second didn't seem to feel the scorching touch of the las-bolts in its chest. Belgutei charged to face it, his blade singing as it met the ork's in a vicious parry, then flicking out to slice open the beast's neck.

Leontus turned away as the ork fell, its clawed hands scrabbling at the blood pumping from its ruined neck. He heard Belgutei's sword sing again as it struck something thick and muscular, then the telltale sound of a head rolling free of its shoulders.

'They're turning,' Belgutei said. 'We need to go.'

'Not yet. I'm not leaving him here.'

Leontus found the cage he had been looking for a few heart-beats later. It was deeper into the ork camp, near its centre and far closer to the bloody melee waged by the rival ork warbands.

'My lord, we have to move!' Belgutei shouted from behind him, but Leontus ignored the Attilan's desperate plea.

Conquest sheared the bolts holding Konstantin captive, his horse standing placidly even as a battle raged on one side and a desperate escape on the other.

'Good to see you, my old friend,' Leontus said, reaching out to run his hand along the shaped ceramite panels that ran the length of Konstantin's neck. The horse's augmetic eyes studied him for a long moment, their unblinking red glare more familiar to Leontus than the golden brown his organic eyes had once been. Konstantin bowed his head in acknowledgement, a harsh exhalation the closest he could come to a friendly snort.

Leontus led Konstantin from his cage and stepped up onto the horse's back, the feeling of his steed's whirring augmetic heartbeat as familiar as his own as he took up the reins built into his horse's facial plating.

'Did you get all the cages open?' he called over to Belgu-tei, who had helped a wounded Catachan up behind him on Nashi's saddle. The Attilan's eyes lingered on Konstantin for a moment too long, a shadow of his revulsion crossing his features before he could mask it.

'We did, but not all of them will escape today,' Belgutei said, turning away to where the orks still fought. 'We would need Chimeras to move those who cannot run.'

Prone forms lay in the dirt within several cages – men and women lost to their wounds before Leontus could liberate them, or those who hadn't survived the orks' rough treatment.

'Then we leave them behind, and may the God-Emperor have mercy on their souls,' Leontus said, even though the words tasted foul on his tongue. Konstantin started forward to the hole in the camp wall, and he busied his mind counting the running Catachans and groups of stumbling Cadians as they all made for the scant safety of the river.

He said a silent prayer of thanks to the God-Emperor and Saint Macharius for their guidance and their generosity. Thirty-six men and women of the Astra Militarum had escaped the Deathskulls camp. He calculated that if only half survived to reach the sanctuary of the cave, he would have enough manpower to begin striking back at the orks.

His mind was occupied with thoughts of strategy and possible routes of attack when Belgutei rode up beside him, the wounded Catachan clinging to his back despite the burns that had blistered half of his torso.

'You owe me a horse, my lord,' Belgutei said solemnly, with a pointed glance at Konstantin's heavily augmented frame.

'I do, and a fast one at that,' Leontus said. 'But Konstantin is mine.'

'Indeed. A lesser man might even ask if all of this was to get your horse back,' Belgutei said, waving a hand to take in the running soldiers.

Leontus held his gaze. 'A good thing that you are not a lesser man, Belgutei. Have Nomak and Rugen lead the survivors up to the plateau. You and I will need to make sure that we aren't followed.'

SEVEN

'Dis i'nt proppa work for proppa orks. Dis is grot work.'

Snazzguts rolled his eyes at Growlkicka's continued grumbling and looked out of the trukk's empty windows over the dead lands either side of the dirt road, a jagged spur on his metal seat digging into his right buttock with each bounce of the cab.

"Ere, try an' keep to da flat bits,' Snazzguts grunted. He'd have to remember to get some extra stuffing for the return trip – squig skin or something he could nick to sort his seat out.

'Wot flat bits?' Growlkicka shouted, letting go of the steering wheel to gesture at the rutted dirt track they were following, and the bikes and escort wagons filled with ladz that bounced out of their seats with every bump.

Snazzguts' eyes were drawn to the trukk's driver's seat under

Growlkicka, at the fresh squig-leather covering. He liked the way it didn't squeal with every rut in the road. Yeah, that'd do nicely for the return trip.

'Bloody 'Ead Nobz givin' orders like they's running da Waaagh! now,' said Growlkicka, continuing his grumbling.

'They sez Irontoof's gone kicked it on his kroozer,' Snazzguts said, the beginnings of a plan forming in his bored mind. 'You could argue it wiv 'em, I s'pose?'

'An' wot, get krumped like Mogga's Mob?' Growlkicka half laughed, before narrowing his eyes at his co-driver, his knuckles popping audibly over the clatter of the engine as he gripped the wheel. 'Dis is my trukk, Snazzguts. Don't be gettin' no ideas.'

'I wasn't finkin' nuffin' like dat, 'onest,' Snazzguts said truthfully. He hadn't thought about taking the trukk for himself, but he was a good driver, and he wouldn't need to sit in the passenger seat if he was driving...

'I likes my 'ead where it is,' Growlkicka said, his dour mind already back on his earlier rant. 'Wot 'Ead Nobz is doin's not natural. It's not orky.'

Snazzguts sighed and looked out of the cracked remains of the windscreen, resting his heavy jaw on his fist as he watched the biker escorts start to struggle in the loose mud. Their wheels had become mired in the brown slurry, and even the tracked ones were having trouble; fountains of silty muck were being sprayed up into the riders' faces with little effect, whilst the boyz in the other wagons jeered and laughed. They wouldn't be laughing when they passed Mad Red's camp in a bit, or at least what remained of it.

"Ere, why's it muddy round dis way? We'z not even close to da river yet,' Growlkicka said as the steering wheel juddered in his hands. Once it was back under control, he stuck his head out of the window to check that their load was still on the back of the trukk. Snazzguts did the same, ignoring the jeering shouts from the biker boyz as he craned his neck to see.

'It's still dere!' he shouted over the rumbling clatter of the engine.

He slid back into his seat and the jagged spur reminded him of its presence with a stab of sudden pain in his backside, but that wasn't why he cried out.

'STOP!' Snazzguts bellowed, but Growlkicka was still half-out of his window, and hadn't seen that the wagon full of boyz had come to a halt as its tyres dug wet channels in the flooded ground.

They hit the rear of the wagon at speed, crumpling the thick metal sheeting that served as the engine cover and spraying the remains of the windscreen over the boyz in the back. Snazzguts was thrown forward, his shout of anger and pain lost beneath the screeching boom of the two vehicles colliding.

Something was hissing loudly as Snazzguts shook his head to clear the ringing from his ears, and thin white smoke was pluming from the crumpled panels that housed the trukk's engine. One of his teef had come loose in the crash, so he pried it out and stashed it away in a pocket for later spending.

'Why da zoggin' hell have dey stopped!?' Growlkicka roared, pulling shards of broken glass from his forearms between taloned fingers. 'Look what dey've done to my–'

Growlkicka's face and chest were chewed apart by a sudden flurry of stabbing lights, just as the boyz in the back were scythed down by a withering hail of hard rounds that rang the wagon's bed like a bell. Snazzguts dropped to the cab's floor, scrabbling for his shoota with one hand and covering his head with the other, as his rickety, creaking, buttock-stabbing chair was peppered with scorch marks that stank of ozone.

He knew that smell.

"UMIES!' he roared, and kicked off the trukk's door as he grabbed his good choppa. He thought all the humies had been rounded up or krumped, but he knew the tang of their fancy little light guns. No self-respecting ork would resort to one of those puny toys over a proper shoota, and only a mad lad would attack one of the 'Ead Nobz convoys.

He dropped to the swampy earth in a splash of brackish mud, his war cry already on his lips.

An ork jumped out of the transport's cab brandishing a heavy blade, its cry cut short as two heavy bolter rounds took it high in the chest. The mass-reactive shells detonated on impact, spraying the side of its wagon with chunks of flesh and skin, as the ork burst apart like an overripe fruit, ending its impotent charge before it had begun.

'Nomak, tell the bolter team to hold their fire. They're wasting ammunition,' Leontus said.

Belgutei watched from his saddle as Nomak tore off down the slope to the hidden heavy bolter emplacement halfway up the rise, covered by camouflage netting that the Catachans had rigged up overnight. With no working vox-set or commbeads, the Lord Solar used the Attilans to carry his orders to his troops; it wasn't work that any of them relished.

Nashi pawed at the ground, as eager as her rider to be charging at the enemy rather than sitting back in reserve. Or she didn't share Belgutei's desire to spill ork blood, and was simply uncomfortable so close to the Lord Solar's machine horse; either way, she was on edge and Belgutei shared her unease.

The Lord Solar sat only a few feet away atop Konstantin, the cybernetic creature standing statuesque as the ambush played out on the sodden ground below it.

'Sound the close assault,' Leontus ordered. Belgutei drew his hunting horn and blew a long, mournful note that set Nashi to stamping, but he held her firm.

Soldiers broke cover across the rise, throwing off their camouflage and scrambling out of concealed foxholes to charge at the remaining orks with an array of improvised weapons: the shattered shafts of spent hunting lances were wielded like spears, and scavenged ork choppas were carried in hands far too small to effectively use them. But still they charged, brave men and women of the Lord Solar's personal army who weren't lucky enough to be given a working lasgun recovered from the landing fields.

Belgutei watched as they hacked at wounded orks. He watched their individual battles with the xenos that had escaped the first volleys. He watched them die.

He watched because he knew better than to ask the Lord Solar for permission to ride down with Rugen and lend their lances to the cause. It was the third ambush he had watched from a distance close enough that he could smell the singed ork-flesh, unable to add his own kills to the death tally. The Lord Solar wanted Belgutei and his riders close by, away from the fighting, but gave no explanation for holding them back.

Of course, he didn't have to give his reasons. He was the Lord Solar.

Then, only a couple of minutes after it had begun, the ambush was over. Ork bodies lay dead across the churned mud and blood, the river's redirected water turning the dry ground into a deep slurry that the xenos had driven into without a second thought. Their wrecked vehicles bled smoke into the sky in roiling ink-black columns, their engines shot through by heavy bolter shells and tyres punctured by las-fire so they would be all but useless to the enemy.

'Rugen, tell Sergeant Raust to destroy his earthworks at the river. They've done their job,' the Lord Solar ordered. Then he motioned for Belgutei to follow as he nudged Konstantin towards the ambush site.

'Three days of digging earthworks for a few minutes' shooting,' Belgutei said as they rode, 'and like that, it's over. It is not a way of war I think I'll ever get used to, my lord.'

'Think of it as three days of preparation for the perfect strike,' the Lord Solar replied, raising his hand to acknowledge a pair of saluting Cadians as he passed. 'Or, as close to perfect as we can get with what we have. It's another weapon denied to the enemy, which means one fewer to face when we take the space port.'

The Lord Solar dismounted next to where the fallen were being laid out, ready to be removed from the battlefield. Belgutei watched as he made a quiet prayer over the three bodies as the living set about their work, stripping the orks of anything useful and destroying whatever wasn't. It had to look like another ork warband were responsible, just like the previous ambushes, which meant recovering their own dead and burning everything else. That day's tally was two Cadians and a Catachan, the highest death toll of the three ambushes they'd carried out so far. It wasn't a high price to pay for over twenty xenos dead, but it was a cost they could ill-afford.

'Anything usable?' Belgutei called out to a grey-haired Cadian who was busy examining the humongous cannon at the centre of the ork convoy.

'Not unless your horse can carry this monster,' Sergeant Andersson called back. The cannon was at least twenty feet long, the barrel discoloured by heat bloom beneath a thick layer of soot and oil, and chambered for shells that must have been half the height of a man. It was a terrifying weapon, almost certainly scavenged from a voidship of some kind, and Belgutei was glad that it wouldn't be used against him or his men.

'I'm already carrying the heavy bolter, I'm not sure I can take both.'

'A shame,' Andersson said with an exaggerated shrug, and motioned for his men to start bringing forth the ork guns and ammunition. They'd soon found that the xenos' battered and ramshackle firearms were all but useless in human hands, so used them to spike the cannons instead.

Belgutei left Andersson and his men to their work, jamming the ork weapons into the cannon's barrel, and made for where the Lord Solar stood watching the northern horizon. His arms were folded across his golden breastplate, one gloved finger tapping his chin as he considered the empty ground before him.

'We're almost ready, my lord,' Belgutei said, swaying in the saddle as Nashi picked her way through the thick mire.

'Good,' he said absently. 'Any usable weapons?'

Belgutei turned in his saddle with a grunt; his leg was healing well, but the ork's teeth had bitten deep and the wounds still pained him. The meagre loot recovered from the convoy had been piled next to the dead, consisting of some stikkbombs, promethium cans, and ammunition that would be broken down for explosives – hardly enough to give them victory overnight, but it was better than nothing.

'None that we can use. It might be time for us to range out to the landing fields again, my lord.'

'I will consider it,' the Lord Solar said.

Belgutei understood his reluctance. Once they had liberated the survivors of the landing site, the next challenge had been to turn them into an effective fighting force, and that meant arming them. Belgutei had been at a loss as to how it might be possible to do so, but the Lord Solar hadn't hesitated in leading a night mission to the site of the massacre in order to recover weapons from the dead. Arnetz had accompanied the Lord Solar, alongside a few other Catachans who were fit enough to take along. Belgutei had remained behind in the cavern, and it had been a tense night's wait for the scavenging party's return. But return they did, with less than a dozen lasguns and a heavy bolter strapped to Konstantin's flank. Arnetz and the Catachans hadn't spoken about what it had taken to recover the few weapons that they had brought back, and Belgutei didn't have the stomach to ask.

The Catachan medicae was tending to a wounded Cadian away from the road, but her eyes flicked over to the three dead soldiers as she wrapped the wounded woman's mangled arm.

'More lasguns may mean fewer deaths, my lord,' Belgutei said quietly.

'More lasguns means more ammunition,' the Lord Solar said. 'Ammunition that we don't have.' He stepped back into Konstantin's saddle as if his limbs were made of lead, and Belgutei thought it was more than the weight of the mud on his boots holding him down.

'We're ready to blow the cannon, my lord,' Andersson called from the weapon's trailer, and the Lord Solar ordered the last few of his men away from the ork vehicles.

'Fire in the hole!'

Andersson leaped from the cannon's trailer, throwing aside the pin of an ork stikkbomb as he took cover behind the trukk's cab. The explosive set off a chain reaction deep in the belly of the cannon's barrel, and it belched flame, giving Belgutei a frightening vision of what it might have looked like to see the weapon fired in anger.

With a sound that was both a thunderous clap and the clang of a tolling bell, the cannon's skin split in a spider's web of cracks and it slid from its moorings, shattering the trailer's rudimentary suspension as it dropped into the mud in a spray of dirty water. Nashi fretted at the sudden sound, but Konstantin seemed entirely unaffected, and the Lord Solar nudged him into motion, leaving Belgutei to calm his horse as he glanced back to the north.

He didn't need to know what the Lord Solar was thinking as he made to follow, because it was on his mind too: for each of the convoys they ambushed and destroyed, still more were being sent, and the rewards for the Imperials were slim. They couldn't stop the flow of weapons by ambushing a convoy every few days, nor were the convoys providing enough materiel to build an arsenal strong enough to assault the xenos strongholds.

But as he helped the Catachans strap the heavy bolter to Nashi's saddle a few minutes later, a troubling thought nagged at the back of his mind, one that he was sure the Lord Solar had already considered.

If they couldn't stop the flow of weapons, how were they ever going to retake the space port?

EIGHT

'We're down to about fifty rounds for the heavy bolter and two charge packs each for the lasguns, my lord.'

'Only two?' the Lord Solar said in surprise.

'They're degrading faster than expected. The more we charge them in the fires, the fewer shots we're getting per pack.'

Arnetz watched Andersson giving his after-action report from her usual spot behind the Lord Solar, leaning against the slick limestone of the cave wall as the Lord Solar held court on the upper level of the cavern. She chewed on her day's ration of dried leporidae meat while the others spoke, washing away the gamey taste with a slug from her canteen after each bite.

'We need more fire discipline from your shooters. Kill shots only, wherever possible,' the Lord Solar said with a shake of his head. 'And restrict the heavy bolter to short bursts into massed targets. It's a suppression weapon after all.'

'I will convey that to the men, my lord,' Andersson said. A muscle in his jaw flexed as he stood straight-backed and rigid, but the old Cadian was disciplined enough not to show his disappointment that the Lord Solar had found fault in his soldiers.

'Also convey that they're doing an excellent job, sergeant. More than I could ever have asked of them, but we still need more if we're going to survive.'

'I'd be happy to, my lord,' Andersson said, the shadow of a smile tugging at the corner of his mouth.

'Very good. Sergeant Raust, where are we on the ration situation?'

'We are averaging around ten of the leporidae per day in the snares, but gathering fish from the lake is becoming difficult due to the increased aerial patrols,' Raust reported in his clipped Krieg accent.

'We've noticed increased patrols too,' Arnetz said. 'My scouts have reported more activity around the space port during the day, occasionally ranging further into the mountains.'

'Are they beginning to suspect we're here, do you think?' Belgutei asked the group at large.

Raust shook his head. 'They would have attacked by now.'

'We're lucky that they haven't found this place already,' Andersson added.

'There's nothing for them here, as far as they know. It's difficult to access, remote, and devoid of anything to fight,' the Lord Solar said, cutting their discussion short. 'I appreciate your efforts, Sergeant Raust. Do what you can to increase rations whilst keeping us concealed.'

'Yes, my lord.'

'Sergeant Arnetz, do you have anything to add?'

Arnetz pushed off the wall and saluted the Lord Solar, her new rank still strange to hear spoken aloud. 'Nothing yet on the private matter we discussed. Our scouts on the plateau reported that the abandoned Deathskulls prison camp had been occupied by a small warband last night, but they'd gone by this morning. Scavengers, most likely.'

Andersson raised a questioning eyebrow at the mention of a private matter, but she ignored him.

'Very good, thank you, sergeant,' the Lord Solar said. 'If there's nothing else, I suggest–'

'I have a matter that I believe we should discuss, my lord,' Belgutei said.

Andersson and Arnetz shared a quick glance, but Raust's response was unreadable beneath his respirator mask. Even after days in his company, she still found the one-armed Krieg sergeant disconcerting – his stoicism made him almost statuesque, and with his face covered, he was a hard man to read. The others she understood, but Raust remained a mystery.

'Perhaps we should speak privately?'

'It's relevant to everyone here, my lord.'

'Then please continue,' the Lord Solar said, and gestured for Belgutei to speak.

'I must ask if we are any closer to attacking the space port? With each ambush we are diminished and the takings are… small, to say the least,' Belgutei said.

'Each cannon we destroy is another weapon denied to the enemy. That is progress in itself.' There was a note of warning in the Lord Solar's tone. 'I assure you, I have not lost sight of the end goal. I will tell you when the time is right, but for now, I must ask you all to hold your nerve for a little longer.' He looked at each of them in turn, his jaw set as he sought to reassure them.

'In that case, my lord, I must again request that my men and I be allowed to play a more active role.'

'You are performing the role I need you to perform,' the Lord Solar said, and Arnetz silently begged Belgutei to hear the finality in his tone. The Attilan was stubborn, but he didn't seem to understand that he was testing the limits of the Lord Solar's patience.

'With respect, my lord, I disagree. We could be doing more, if not in your ambushes then to scout the camps we spotted to the west and north-west. If you would but allow us to–'

'Enough,' the Lord Solar barked, and Belgutei fell silent. 'This isn't up for discussion – you and your riders are where I need you.'

Belgutei's head dropped beneath the full weight of the Lord Solar's attention, his jaw working as he bit down on his response. She felt for him in that moment, understanding his desire for he and his men to be more than glorified bodyguards and messengers for the Lord Solar, but restricted to that limited role as others fought, scouted, or in Raust's case, hunted for food.

'I am sorry, my lord.' Belgutei said eventually, but he did not raise his head.

'You are dismissed, all of you,' the Lord Solar said with a wave of his hand, turning away from his sergeants both new and experienced. They each offered an aquila salute, Raust's one hand placed over his heart, then departed for the lower level of the cave. Arnetz looked back to see the Lord Solar removing the Radiant Helm, his once close-cropped dark hair glinting with new silver growth around his temples. It was sometimes hard to remember that he was over a century old, kept strong by a regime of rejuvenat treatments and subtle augmetics, but she was starting to see the old veteran behind the meticulously crafted facade that was the Lord Solar.

'You're following your orders, Belgutei,' Andersson said. 'No one thinks less of you or your men for that.'

'I do,' Belgutei retorted, and strode away to where Nomak tended the horses near the mouth of the cave. The other Attilan met him expectantly, his expression darkening as Belgutei shook his head and began talking in low tones that didn't carry over the sound of the river.

Arnetz and Andersson shared a look.

'He's in a difficult position,' Andersson said quietly.

'We all are,' Arnetz replied, glancing at Raust. The Krieg man didn't offer an opinion but made for a corner of the cavern where his command, the other wounded soldiers who weren't able to fight, sorted through their various stores.

'I don't think our quartermaster approves of Belgutei's questions,' Andersson said.

'I don't think he approves of any questions, least of all when they're directed at the Lord Solar,' Arnetz replied, smiling. She liked the old Cadian; his humour was dark and dry, which made him far less gloomy than the Cadians she'd served with before and a much better conversationalist than Belgutei or Raust.

'He's holding them back for a reason,' Andersson said as Belgutei and Nomak made for the cavern's mouth, still deep in conversation. 'Though in fairness, I don't know what I'd do in his position either.'

'You'd follow orders, just like I would,' Arnetz sighed.

'What is it?'

'It's not just Belgutei who's in a difficult position.' Arnetz nodded to the upper level of the cavern, where the Lord Solar stood alone. 'He had legions of Titans, Knight households, and a thousand regiments of the Astra Militarum, not to mention the Collegiate Astrolex and his private army of logisticians, data-scryers, savants and tacticians. Now all he has is us, and we're not exactly a substitute for any of it.'

Andersson considered her words for a few moments, watching as the Lord Solar turned and disappeared in the shadows towards the rear of the cavern.

'You know, I used to know an officer in the Vostroyan First-born. Went by the name of Yonas Sabavich Kuriaki Aleksandrov.'

Arnetz laughed. 'That's a mouthful.'

'You're not wrong. He was a strange man, with some really odd ideas, but I remember he once said that the Lord Solar is unlucky to live in the time of the primarch's return, forced to build his legend in the shadow of the Lord Regent's crusade.'

'That's straying very close to heresy.'

'I'd say it's on the borderline, but he wasn't wrong. Lord Solar Leontus has come the closest to matching the achievements of Saint Macharius of any Lord Solar since,' Andersson said. He gave Arnetz a reassuring bump on the shoulder. 'We're in safe hands.'

As Arnetz left the cavern a few minutes later, Andersson's words buzzed around her mind like a fly in a field tent. She believed in the Lord Solar's tactical knowledge and his skills; after all, every ambush he had devised had been an unmitigated success, denying weapons to the enemy with minimal losses to his own forces. But…

But.

The kernel of doubt still niggled at the back of her mind like a scrap of stringy meat stuck between two teeth, seemingly as impossible to remove as it was to ignore. He was still a man, a human who was as fallible as anyone else – the massacre on the landing fields was testament to that fact, and she seemed to be the only one who noticed the intense pressure wearing down the Lord Solar with each daily report.

Then there was Belgutei. She understood Belgutei's frustrations, just as she understood the Lord Solar's caution, but the Attilan was pushing in the wrong direction. He didn't worship the Lord Solar in the same unquestioning way that Raust did, nor did he have Andersson's active belief that they were fighting for the greatest living commander of the Astra Militarum. He didn't even have her quiet trust that the Lord Solar was their best chance for survival, if not victory, on Fortuna Minor.

The Attilan was a problem that she did not have the answer to.

'Sarge,' a short Catachan said with a nod of his head as she passed. She had been so consumed by her thoughts that she'd walked almost to the end of the slot canyon, and came to a halt overlooking the plateau and the glistening surface of the lake.

'Barratt,' she said with a nod of her own. 'Anything to report?'

'Nah, just that I am tired and hungry,' Barratt said with a white-toothed grin. 'Those Attilan lads tore out pretty fast, though. I feel bad for whatever gets in their way.'

'So do I.'

'I saw what one of those melta lances did to a Leman Russ once. Bloody big bang it was, I said to–'

'Barratt!' Arnetz hissed to quiet him and dropped to one knee, pointing out across to the east of the lake where two figures had appeared by the waterline. 'Magnoculars.'

Barratt slid the lanyard from around his thick neck and passed her his battered magnoculars; one of the lenses was shattered, but the machine spirit still responded with a little coaxing. She raised them to her eyes and zoomed in on the figures – too broad to be Cadian or Attilan, but too far away to be sure if they were Catachan or ork.

She recognised their faces immediately as those of her scouts, both returning unhurt. A deeply held tension was released, and she let out a long, slow breath.

'Barratt, go and tell the Lord Solar that I need to speak to him about our private matter.'

'What did you find?'

'It's a downed voidship all right, a few miles to the east of the plateau. Much too large to be a lander, though with the state it's in I couldn't say whether it was one of ours or theirs, my lord.'

Leera and Mattis both stood to stiff attention before the Lord Solar as they explained their findings, hidden away in the very back of the cavern. They had knelt like subjects before their king at first, but Arnetz had long since learned that the Lord Solar had little patience for courtly etiquette. At least, not the rough version that the Catachans were capable of.

'If you had to guess?' he pressed.

'I'd say that it was an ork kroozer,' Leera said after a moment's hesitation. 'If it was an Imperial vessel then it's been messed up pretty badly.'

'Enemy disposition?' Arnetz asked.

'There was quite a bit of activity, but it's well over a hundred from what we could see from the outside. They've already stripped most of the guts out,' Mattis said.

'And the approach? Is there a way to get close?'

'Open ground for the most part, no cover to speak of. We'd be spotted before we got within a mile of the walls,' Leera said. 'It's a few miles clear of the plateau, so we might make it there and back in a night if we were on foot.'

The Lord Solar nodded, running his tongue over his teeth as he considered the scouts' report. Arnetz watched him as his mind worked over the problem, his eyes narrowing almost imperceptibly as he came to a decision.

'I need you to go back,' he said at last. 'Get as close as you can and scout the perimeter after nightfall – around the entire downed ship if you can. I need an idea of enemy numbers and descriptions of any distinctive xenos that you see. Is that understood?'

Arnetz's stomach clenched. To stray too close to the ork lines was incredibly dangerous, even for experienced scout and ambush troops like Catachans.

'Yes, my lord,' the scouts said in unison.

'My lord, I request permission to go along with troopers Leera and Mattis,' Arnetz said before she could stop herself.

'Granted,' the Lord Solar replied without hesitation, which took her by surprise. 'Take someone else along too. Two teams of two should cut down the time you need.'

'Yes, my lord.'

'Go prepare,' Arnetz said. 'We travel light. Dismissed.'

Leera and Mattis both made the sign of the aquila and handed over their magnoculars before departing, clearly exhilarated to have been in the Lord Solar's confidence.

'It looks like your suspicions were correct – the weapons are coming from the downed ship, my lord,' Arnetz said as the troopers disappeared down the slope onto the main cavern floor. The Lord Solar had asked her to send out two scouts after the ambush that morning, but not before she had sworn not to tell anyone else about where they were going.

'Perhaps, perhaps not. It's not useful information unless we can find a weakness that we can exploit,' he said.

She had the distinct impression that the Lord Solar was juggling a number of competing thoughts, and none of them brought him any solace.

'Make sure that you return, sergeant, even if you are the only one that does. We need our medicae as much as we need this information.'

* * *

Leera was right. Whatever the downed ship had been before it crashed on Fortuna Minor, it was unrecognisable now.

It had ploughed into the ground at such speed that the impact crater was several miles wide, though the winds that howled across the open plains had worn down the crater's lip to a low incline since its landing. Its prow was buried deep into the earth, a full half of the ship left protruding like a splinter from the planet's skin. The leviathan's back had been broken upon impact, folding the spine of the vessel upon itself like an inverted 'V'. Its ancient bones had shattered, leaving a blackened forest of rusting metal spars that jutted towards the sky, each hundreds of feet long.

Arnetz lay flat on her belly on the sun-bleached grass, her skin streaked with a crude camo-paint substitute made from charcoal dust and a quantity of engine grease she had pilfered from the victims of the first ambush. It still had a slight smell of burned wood and sharp chems, but not enough that she could afford to go without it even at night. She watched as sparks danced across the ship's outer hull, rappelling orks shouting to each other in their crude tongue as they cut usable chunks from the armour and loosened sections of plating. Tons of alloy and plasteel dropped hundreds of feet to slam into the earth with force enough that Arnetz felt the ground tremble from the crater's edge. Spot-lumens bathed the craft's exposed innards where the orks had gouged deep into its structure, revealing yet more xenos working within.

'Yeah, this is the fragging place,' Arnetz muttered to Barratt, and pointed down to the well-lit camp that had been erected around the ship's base. A crane was straining to lift a cannon onto a trailer attached to an ork trukk, the massive barrel swinging haphazardly as the xenos shouted apparently contradictory orders to the operator.

'We could've done with a little more cloud cover if we're getting this close,' Barratt whispered, the whites of his eyes the only visible part of him beneath his own layers of charcoal and grease. Fortuna Minor's twin moons were both shining brightly amongst the stars, which had made their infiltration far more difficult than it might have been.

'Can't make it too easy, can we,' she said with a confidence she didn't quite feel. 'Come on, we need to scout the rear.'

She led Barratt down into the crater in a crouch, the pair keeping low as they ran across the heat-scarred dirt in an oblique line and staying clear of the globe of light hanging around the ork camp. Her eyes were on the camp's high walls and the shadow of the ship as they moved, waiting for the moment a savage throat would scream an alarm and they would be caught.

It was exhilarating.

They saw fewer and fewer signs of organised xenos activity the further around the perimeter they scouted, but flickers of movement in the deepest shadows around the ship's base told her that they weren't the only things creeping around in the dark.

'Movement – down!' she hissed as a shape loomed to their left, followed by light footsteps crunching across scorched dirt. She lowered herself smoothly to the ground, sliding her knife from its sheath as she readied herself.

A high, thin voice called out into the darkness, putting Arnetz in mind of a child seeking reassurance.

Arnetz barely breathed, but her heart hammered with sudden adrenaline. It was beating so hard that she was sure the creature must be able to feel it through the ground, but it just called out again into the dark, then once more, the sense of threat now somewhat undermined by the fearful wobble that coloured its garbled syllables. It was moving away from the ship to their left, and Arnetz caught its silhouette against the distant light of the camp. It was a grot – a two-foot-tall creature with large, pointed ears and a long, hooked nose. Her *Infantryman's Uplifting Primer* said they were an ork subspecies, but the larger brutes seemed to have cast this runt out into the night.

Yet again, the grot called out, a note of warning clear in its voice.

Even if it didn't have a weapon, its voice was going to attract attention before long, and Arnetz couldn't allow that. She rose from the ground and crept towards the diminutive creature.

She was close enough to hear it draw in a breath in preparation for another shout when she struck.

Arnetz clamped her hand over the grot's mouth, feeling no lips, only twin rows of dagger-sharp teeth that instantly gnashed at her silencing grip. Her other hand brought the serrated edge of her knife to the creature's throat, and with one swift slice its body went limp. She dropped the severed head next to the body and sheathed her blade before moving off again to the east with Barratt following in her wake.

They circled around to the rear of the downed ship, where another structure perched, a dangling limb still connected to the front half by sinews of twisted gantries and scraps of hull plating.

'That looks promising,' Barratt breathed, moving in close to point at three globes of true darkness, flattened circles that seemed to swallow the dim light cast by the twin moons above.

'The engines,' Arnetz said with a nod. There was no sign of the orks working on the fallen tail of the ship, despite the easier pickings and powerful resources it must have offered.

'Why aren't they cannibalising it?'

'Because there aren't any weapons on the back of this ship,' Arnetz said, as realisation struck. 'Come on, we need to find Leera and Mattis. We've found our way in.'

NINE

As dawn broke over Fortuna Minor, Leontus stood with the sentries posted at the mouth of the slot canyon that led to the cavern. He watched the eastern horizon for sign of Arnetz's scouting party and the west for Belgutei and his riders, who still hadn't returned from their impromptu and unapproved ride the night before.

He sighed and pinched the bridge of his nose in an attempt to ward off the headache that was already firing warning shots of pain behind his eyes. He'd been unable to sleep and the long hours were wearing him down, his mind still racing with possible stratagems and counter-stratagems based on whatever Arnetz may have found. None addressed the fact that his fledgling force was too small and too badly armed to have any real impact on the ork forces, nor the fact that he had mismanaged Belgutei into riding out with his men. He hadn't forbidden it, nor ordered the Attilans to remain in the cavern; that was his mistake, and it may well have cost him dearly.

'My lord, figures on the eastern bank,' one of the sentries called, pointing out over the water to a small group moving quickly towards the cavern. It appeared that Arnetz would be the first to return.

'Tell Sergeant Arnetz to see me when she's back. And send word if there's any sign of the Attilans.'

Sergeant Arnetz's face was a mask of sweat beneath the thick daubing of improvised camo-paint, but her evident fatigue had no impact on the precise report she delivered to Leontus, Andersson and Raust.

She used a sharpened chunk of river stone to scratch an outline of the downed ship and its surroundings onto a patch of dry limestone to the rear of the cave, explaining each element as she set out her suggested plan.

'If we were able to circle around the rear, where the orks are least concentrated, we might be able to infiltrate through the engine cowling to the heart of the ship,' she explained, scratching a long, curved line into the stone. 'We're short of guns, but we have explosives – even if we don't destroy the ship itself, we can set back their operation there.'

'If we could find the magazine…' Andersson mused.

'Unlikely, but not impossible,' Leontus said with a nod. 'Munitions are often the first resources looted by the orks, but if anything remains of the ship's magazine it could be detonated. Did you get any idea of the enemy numbers, Arnetz?'

'We stopped counting after one hundred and fifty.'
'Ah.'

Andersson let out a long sigh and turned away from the

scratched map. That was a large warband, far larger than any they had dared to attack on the convoy routes so far.

'We can't take that on with what we have. It'd be suicide,' he said.

'If we're to stop the flow of weapons into the space port, then we need to destroy them at their source,' Leontus said. 'Do not think of it as a ship – it is a weapons stockpile, a vital part of the enemy infrastructure that we must deny them. Every day that the orks strip materiel from it is a step backward for us.'

'My plan would work,' Arnetz said. 'Infiltration is our best option. If we can get some small teams inside–'

'No,' Andersson interrupted. 'You counted over a hundred and fifty from the outside, and there could be the same again inside, if not more.'

Leontus waited, watching the three sergeants to see which would come to the only feasible option – the one that he had been considering since Arnetz had finished drawing her plans.

'A diversionary attack,' Raust said eventually, his voice soft and muffled through his respirator. 'We draw the bulk of the enemy forces away, reducing resistance within the structure.'

It was quiet for a moment as Andersson stared in surprise.

'That's suicide,' he said.

'I volunteer to lead the diversionary attack with the other wounded,' Raust said without hesitation, ignoring Andersson's shocked expression.

'What? No, we've not agreed–'

The Lord Solar nodded. 'Thank you, Sergeant Raust. I will take it under consideration.'

'My lord, you can't–'

'Enough,' Leontus said, cutting Andersson's protests short. 'There are other preparations that we need to make before we can launch this attack. Belgutei mentioned two camps to the west – I want them both scouted and assessed for any captives. Arnetz, you go tonight. Andersson, prepare your men to head south to Bruke Fields. We can't take on the orks with sticks and stones, we need real weapons.'

The sound of steel-shod hooves on rock clattered through the cave mouth, which drew all of their attention away from the maps to the cavern floor. Belgutei rode in with Csaba on the rear of his saddle, the younger Attilan's horse given over to carrying bundles of lasguns and a long-barrelled auto-cannon, whilst Rugen and Nomak's horses were heavily laden with yet more weapons and belts of shells.

The troops began to clap as the Attilans pulled on their reins, Nashi circling nervously at the unfamiliar sound. In her saddle, Belgutei looked up at Leontus with defiance in his eyes.

'We brought much-needed weapons and other equipment.'

'You left during daylight hours, without orders, and could have led the enemy right to us.'

'If we'd been seen, then we would already be dead. With everything we were carrying, we couldn't exactly make a quick escape.'

'But you could have been, Belgutei. We have flown under the enemy's auspex so far, but that was an unnecessary risk.'

Leontus sighed, a dreadful pounding building behind his eyes that could have been fatigue or the restarting of his head-ache. In his younger years, he might have demoted the Attilan in a roared diatribe designed to tear his ego to tatters, or even threatened to shoot him if he set a toe out of line again. In his decades as the supreme commander of all Astra Militarum forces in the Segmentum Solar, he had been forced to duel, execute, demote, reassign, and retire more inept and hysterical soldiers than he cared to admit; but Belgutei was neither inept nor hysterical. When he looked at the Attilan, he saw a man who wished to reaffirm that he was useful to the cause – not for the sake of impressing his superior officers, but to prove it to himself.

That was why Leontus knew he had made a mistake in holding the Attilans back from the fight, even if telling them why he had kept them in reserve would have been far worse. He had held them back too long and too tightly, and now he had to deal with the consequences.

'You're a damned fool, Belgutei. Tell me what you did.'

Leontus listened as Belgutei gave his report in the broadest strokes: they had ridden south through the dry river canyons and hidden until dark, when they had taken to the landing fields and scavenged everything they could find.

'The autocannon was half-buried beneath a Sentinel walker – we dug it out in the hopes that Sergeant Raust might get it back into workable condition,' he explained.

'And on the field?' Leontus asked.

'My lord?' Belgutei said. 'What do you mean?'

'I mean, you saw the field where we were undone. How did that make you feel?'

Leontus felt a pang of anger at the Attilan's sudden unwillingness to meet his gaze, his eyes downcast as he considered the question.

'It was… not a sight I wish to see again,' he said after a pause.

'Thousands of Astra Militarum dead, all because someone made a mistake,' Leontus said in a low voice, stepping in close enough that he could smell Belgutei's horse on him. 'That someone may even have been me. Regardless, every life lost on that field is tallied against me, because I am responsible for every soldier under my care. Look down at the men and women that you could have killed with your own actions – look.'

Leontus pointed to the troopers on the cavern floor, busy unloading and inspecting the weapons that Belgutei had brought back.

'You don't want them on your conscience when you go to meet the God-Emperor.'

'No, my lord,' Belgutei said softly.

'Then start thinking with your mind and not your pride.'

Belgutei nodded but didn't make to leave.

'Was there something else?'

'We found tracks, my lord,' Belgutei said. 'Hoofprints leading to the north-west, away from the space port towards the plains.'

'Attilans?' Leontus said, thinking aloud, the information sparking new plans and contingencies in his mind. 'Could you tell how many?'

'There were too many ork prints muddying the ground to tell, but there may still be some of my people out there, my lord. Captives, but still alive.'

Leontus regarded the younger Attilan then, looking past the sleep-deprived horseman to the warrior beneath. He stood taller than he had in days, invigorated by his discovery despite the horrors his people would endure under the orks' care.

'If there are other Attilans alive on Fortuna Minor, I promise that we will find them, Belgutei. When the time is right.'

'Thank you, my lord. That is all I can ask.'

As Belgutei descended the slope to a clamour of congratulations from the gathered troops below, Leontus wondered if he had finally met the man the Rough Rider had been before Bruke Fields almost broke him.

* * *

It took another two days to gather the information he needed after Belgutei's triumphant return – two days of reports of greater ork activity to the south-west around the space port and deliveries of weaponry and components being driven in from across the plains. Leontus dispatched scouts to watch the road that wound from the downed ship to the east, around the southern foothills, and on to the west, noting the scale and frequency of the convoys that skirted the foothills. The information gathered across those two days told him that time was no longer on the Imperials' side.

'The enemy activity is gaining a cohesion that the orks rarely achieve without a single, unified purpose,' he told Arnetz, Raust, Belgutei, and Andersson at midday on the second day, the layouts of two new camps scratched into the rock wall beside the Catachan's sketch of the downed ship encampment.

'A new warboss, maybe? Or an alliance between groups?' Andersson suggested, but Leontus shook his head.

'There's no way to know. While we no longer have the advantage of their in-fighting, we can instead exploit their complacency,' Leontus said, and pointed to each of the new drawings in turn. 'This camp is due west of the plateau, this camp to the north-west. Both have been scouted and contain a large number of prisoners being used for who knows what. Arnetz, if you would?'

Arnetz stepped forward and began relaying the reports she had collated alongside her Catachan scouts, detailing enemy strength, disposition, and the estimated number of prisoners in each camp.

'The western camp, designated Tertius, is the smaller camp. In the region of twenty orks holding thirty captives – a small enough number that we can wipe out the xenos and liberate the prisoners. The north-western camp is a different story,' she said, and moved to the second outline. 'Designation Secundus. It's much larger, with walls, vehicles, and a bigger garrison, but more captives too.'

'Before Fortuna Minor, I didn't think orks took captives,' Belgutei said. 'I don't understand – why take captives at all?'

'Labour,' Andersson said, his expression cold. 'Entertainment. Food.'

'We're taking both Tertius and Secundus tonight,' Leontus said, steering the conversation away from ork barbarism. 'We're collecting our army tonight. Tomorrow night we use it to destroy Ultima.'

The sergeants looked confused for a moment, then turned to the outline of the downed ship, under which a designation symbol had been scratched.

'In the God-Emperor's name,' Raust said.

Konstantin limped up the rise, a servo in his right foreleg spitting sparks with every stuttering step as they made the plateau once more. The grey light of pre-dawn was yet to be chased away by the coming sunrise, and the morning mists still clung to the lake like a low cloud resting on the water's placid surface.

God-Emperor, Leontus thought, what he would not do for an hour's peace.

Gaunt-eyed men and women trudged past as he turned Konstantin, the freed prisoners of two camps still numbed by their weeks of captivity about to taste a first dawn as free men and women. Some whispered their thanks as they filed past, others offering prayers and benedictions, but most simply kept their heads down as they marched towards their salvation.

At least, some of them did. Leontus knew what the next night would bring, and regretted giving these soldiers their lives with one hand whilst preparing to take them with the other.

'Another successful night, my lord,' Andersson called out as he reached the plateau, his new lasgun hanging from a strap over his shoulder. It was a Krieg-pattern weapon, like most of those Belgutei had recovered, and had seen a great deal of use during the night.

Leontus didn't respond, but continued his count of the force he now had at his disposal. The night had been hard and long, and much of it appeared as a blur as he tried to focus on specific details. What he did recall came in short flashes: slicing an ork in two with his first swing as Konstantin barrelled through a throng of brutes like a missile clad in ceramite and sculpted plasteel; white-hot beams of light lancing past him as he turned, the feeling of grim satisfaction as Andersson's squad picked their shots; a Catachan trooper screaming as he was torn apart by an ork's wrenching claws, and the heat of Sol's Righteous Gaze in his hand as he blasted the xenos apart.

Belgutei's riders had been the hammer blow that had broken the ork lines in Secundus, he knew that much. That was their worth, their true value demonstrated for everyone to see. It was the role he needed them to play in this war, which was why he had held them close for so long, even if they were yet to meet the challenge that he feared was coming.

But for all their martial success, Belgutei's riders had been dealt a bruising blow to their morale: there had been no Attilans amongst the liberated humans, nor any captive horses. They must have been taken further afield, if they still lived at all, and Leontus hoped that fact wouldn't break Belgutei's newfound resolve.

He finished his count and sighed. Seventy-four had survived

the night and the long march back to the cavern. That number might have been far lower, had it not been for Arnetz and her Catachans freeing the captives to aid in their fight in Secundus. But he wished it was higher.

Warmth slowly spread through his back as the sun rose behind him, his taut muscles momentarily relaxing as if he were slipping into a warm bath, but he held himself up in the saddle despite the feeling of lead weights dragging at his limbs. He couldn't appear weak, not in front of the troops, not now.

But as Arnetz led the final few soldiers past him towards the cavern, he suspected that she wasn't convinced.

TEN

Belgutei's legs ached, and not just from the bite wounds that seemed determined not to heal properly. They ached because he was unsure if he'd ever walked so far since the day he learned to ride, when he was a young boy back on Attila.

He'd protested when the Lord Solar set out his plan to take Ultima; after all, he and his men were far better suited to providing the distraction than Raust's group of the walking wounded. Or they could have fulfilled the role given to Andersson's footsloggers, as they'd be better equipped to escape the orks unharmed. He'd even reiterated the old Attilan adage that an Attilan without a horse was as good as dead.

But the Lord Solar would hear none of it, and so Belgutei walked the long miles from the cavern, down through the foothills and across the plains towards Ultima alongside the rest of the Lord Solar's forces, leaving Nashi and the other horses behind. Even the Lord Solar walked, though he was at the front of the column, his golden armour dulled by a liberal coat of the Catachan's camo-paint concoction.

'Is it much further?' Nomak asked.

'Quiet,' Belgutei said, his patience worn thin by the ache in his legs and a growing heat in the small of his back. Rugen's legs were bowed from years in the saddle, and he was already struggling to keep up with the punishing pace of the Catachan march, but hadn't allowed a single word of complaint to pass his scarred lips.

They'd parted ways with Andersson and Raust hours ago, not long after sundown, where their newly reinforced squads had prepared their diversions; they were to take turns drawing out the orks, one retreating as the other attacked from a different direction, keeping the xenos' attention away from Ultima for as long as possible. They'd said their goodbyes and wished each other good luck, and whilst Raust had been as unreadable as ever, Andersson's features had been taut in the moonlight.

Belgutei hoped that he would see them both again.

The twinkling lights of Ultima still seemed to be a long way ahead when the ground changed from grassy plain to fire-scorched dirt, and he was waved forward to the front of the column.

'Three ingress points means three teams,' Leontus murmured, his voice pitched low and soft. 'Belgutei, you and your men are with me. Arnetz, you'll have to split your squad. Look for structural points to plant your charges, but do not engage unless you have to – we're losing the element of surprise after tonight, so let's use every scrap that we have left. In the name of the God-Emperor.'

'In the name of the God-Emperor,' they repeated.

The Lord Solar set off across the hard earth in a crouch, and Belgutei followed with his men in tow. They made for the squashed circles of true darkness beneath the distant lights of plasma cutters and spraying sparks, and the sound of ork voices grew from a distant murmur to a dissonant chorus of insults, barked orders and threats, the floor shaking as hull plates were cut free just as Arnetz had described. The ache in Belgutei's legs was all but forgotten now, smothered beneath a surge of adrenaline as they darted towards the engine cowling, and disappeared into the dark.

Andersson let out a long, slow breath, but found it did little to calm the nervous energy that charged his limbs with the need to move. Not that he'd expected it to. He'd always been this way, even as a Whiteshield, but that feeling would disappear the moment he fired his first shot. Muscle memory would take over, all of the what-ifs and maybes would drop away as dead weight he no longer needed, and there would just be the path ahead.

He lifted the chronometer that the Lord Solar had given him, a masterwork of gold filigree, enamelled facings, and ornate windings behind a face of hair-thin crystal. Its worth was unimaginable, a lifetime's artistry condensed into a sliver of metal that sat in his palm. The hands moved smoothly, inching towards the numeric glyph that the Lord Solar had indicated.

'Two minutes,' he said to the man next to him, one of the few hollow-eyed former prisoners who had been assigned to his squad. The man nodded and turned, passing the word along the line in a whisper that was soon lost to the wind.

He knew that somewhere out there in the dark, Raust would be doing the same.

Andersson took in a long breath and let it out slowly as he watched the seconds tick down.

* * *

The darkness was all-consuming in a way that Arnetz only associated with starships. They were designed to cocoon the living behind layer upon layer of metal and polymers, holding the void out whilst sealing air, light and life within.

As it turned out, they could also hold the inky blackness within themselves just as well.

She felt her way along the inside of the engine exhaust rather than seeing, each footstep carefully tested and placed before she put her weight on it, minimising noise but also slowing their progress down to a crawl. The further into the ship's guts they went, the further they travelled from the little ambient light visible outside. She only gave the order to draw their handheld lumens once they were in complete darkness, clicking hers into life and clipping it to her belt.

Five beams stabbed out in quick succession, illuminating a tangle of pipework and dangling support structures. Her lasgun was up and ready as she scanned the path ahead, but there was no sound, nor the glint of a beady red eye. She exhaled and waved her squad on, hoping that there would be an access point that led into the ship proper; it would be a short mission if they couldn't find their way out of the engines into the enginarium.

Soot caked the floor as they climbed, crunching underfoot like the snows she had once seen on Gadrinax. It had been the first and only time that she had been deployed to an ice world, and she hoped to never feel that cold again. The incline soon steepened, and she and her squad were forced to their hands and knees, climbing the web of pipes and jutting stanchions as their lumens flickered through the entangled metal. They heaved themselves up, their heavy breathing echoing through the cavernous space, until one of the lumen beams suddenly winked out.

Arnetz looked down, her heart in her throat as she waited for the thump of a body smacking into the pipework, the sickening crunch of breaking bone as flesh struck metal.

It didn't come. Instead, there was a sharp crack as something small and metallic shattered, followed by the tinkling of small components bouncing from a hard surface. Arnetz unclipped her lumen and pointed it downward, directly into the soot-smeared face of one of her squad.

'Dropped my damned lumen,' he said apologetically.

Arnetz bit back her response as her lumen beam slid to the soldier's right, where a blackened wheel protruded from the wall.

'Get that hatch open.'

Leontus hauled himself up into the empty doorframe, his sweat prickling his scalp as it ran from beneath the Radiant Helm and onto his forehead. He wiped it away with a soot-blackened hand and turned to help Belgutei up, beads of moisture glistening on the Attilan's face in the dim light.

Their route had taken them straight through the heart of the ship, through access hatches that belonged on Imperial craft and across mushroom-encrusted stone chambers that gave off their own sickly glow. It became almost impossible to orient themselves on their path through the slanted corridors and sloped passageways, but they continued their climb in the hopes that they would find an ammo cache or arsenal large enough to destroy the ship from within.

But they found orks first.

Leontus held a finger to his lips for silence, and pointed up at the end of the passageway; stars were visible through the gaping wound in the ship's hull, silhouetting the outline of a long-limbed ork that was busy coiling a long length of wiring.

It had one booted foot braced against the floor and the other against the wall as it worked in the near-vertical passage, blind to the humans approaching from below it.

Leontus raised a single finger, indicating that Belgutei had one shot. The Attilan nodded silently as he unslung his lasgun, and aimed at the creature's broad back.

A distant rumble resolved into the *thunk thunk thunk* of hard-round impacts, swiftly followed by the roars of a hundred bestial throats and the arrhythmic clatter of return fire. The ork's head shot upwards and it dropped the coiled wiring as it scrambled towards the noise, which was when Belgutei pulled the trigger.

The ork squawked in surprise as much as pain as its knee disintegrated in a flash of heat and light, the echoes of the lasgun's whip-crack report covering Belgutei's hissed curse. It tried to use its useless leg to carry on its climb, but the ruined joint gave way at once and it slipped onto its back, scraping down the deck plating as it hurtled towards where Leontus and Belgutei crouched.

Conquest was out in a flash, the energised blade slamming through flesh and bone and deck plating, and separating the ork's head from its shoulders as the body careened past in a boneless spasm. The xenos' expression went from surprise to anger as it saw the creatures that had killed it, its disembodied head perched precariously on the flat of Conquest's blade.

With a flick of his wrist, Leontus sent the head to join the rest of its body in the darkness below, and watched it tumble away into the ship's depths.

'The distraction has started, we need to move quickly,' Leontus said, and he started the steep climb to the apex of the broken ship.

* * *

Arnetz dropped to one knee at the sound of something heavy rolling across the deck above, slamming into the plating hard enough for dust to trickle down from the overhead pipes before continuing its rumbling path towards the rear of the ship.

'What in the name of Terra…?' she murmured as the echoes moved further away. Whatever it was, it appeared to be travelling down, not up, which meant it wasn't her problem.

'Move up,' she called, 'we must be nearing the apex now.'

Her team moved with practised efficiency, shuffling forward almost on their knees to maximise their contact with the smooth deck plates, digging their boots into whatever footholds they could find whilst keeping their weapons up. The sound of distant battle became ever clearer the further up the slope they travelled, until they were out into the clear air on a gantry made of roughly welded metal plates and riveted supports.

It provided a commanding view over the plains, and of the battle being waged in the inky darkness. Lights flashed and dazzled in clusters before disappearing, only to be replaced by another volley mere inches apart from her perspective, but what must have been hundreds of feet on the ground below. Orks roared and charged as a roiling mass in the gloom, illuminated in staccato bursts of gunfire from their crude shootas.

'God-Emperor protect them,' one of her troopers said.

'God-Emperor protect us too,' she replied. 'We're about to head into the heart of the nest.'

Leontus kicked out at the ork, and it toppled from its suspended perch, dropping its cutting torch as it let out a scream of frustration and plummeted through the night sky. He grabbed the xenos' tool and threw it down the passageway below, where its light illuminated a makeshift staircase that disappeared into the depths of the ship's prow.

'They're still coming, my lord!'

Belgutei's lasgun snapped again and again as he pumped shots into the throng of orks crawling over one another to reach the humans, their mad charge stymied by the narrow bulkheads between the two chambers. Leontus cast one last look through the hole in the ship's hull and gauged how far they had to go.

He drew Sol's Righteous Gaze and added his own fire to Belgutei's.

'There's a staircase thirty yards down the passage – get down and start clearing it. We'll follow when we can,' he shouted over Sol's calamitous report.

An ork in a crudely fashioned welding mask leaped over the bodies of its comrades; Belgutei's las-beams scored red-hot lines in the battered metal but didn't penetrate. Leontus shot it in the lower abdomen, blasting a fist-sized hole in its gut, but still it came on, crawling towards him with a flaming cutting torch still clasped in a clawed hand. A second shot from Sol stopped its faltering advance by disintegrating its skull, welding mask and all.

'Just die!' Belgutei cried, before his lasgun whined empty. 'Reloading!'

'To the abyss with this,' Leontus spat. He drew the frag charge from the small of his back; every member of each infiltration team carried one to help destroy the ship, but they couldn't make any further progress whilst holding the door. He threw it at the orks still clawing at their dead to get at the humans, then shot the canvas-wrapped package.

The concussive blast flung him from his feet, slamming him into a hard surface with enough force to knock the air from his lungs. All sound was lost beneath a high-pitched tinnitus whine for several moments as he scrambled for grip on the slanted floor plates, his numb fingers searching for a handhold that wasn't there, until a hand grabbed his and held him steady.

Belgutei looked down at him, blinking rapidly as his conscious mind fought to process the sudden overload of stimuli.

'Thank you,' Leontus said, his own voice coming to him as if through water.

Belgutei's eyes finally focused, and he smiled through blood-stained teeth. 'Next time, I'll stay with the horses.'

'We'll discuss it,' Leontus said with a laugh as he got his feet beneath him. They were only a short distance from the staircase he had seen below them, and the explosion seemed to have given them the time to make use of it.

They ran down the uneven steps as fast as they could, past missing hull plates and carved-up bulkheads, through low-hanging cables and cavernous voids where the ork cannons had once been mounted. They caught up to Nomak and Rugen at the bottom of the stairway, where the Attilans held open a bulkhead door bathed in artificial light.

'It's the ground level, my lord,' Nomak said, his frantic fingers fumbling a fresh charge pack into his lasgun.

'What is it?' Leontus asked, looking from Nomak to Rugen before hazarding a look through the open doorway.

The space beyond was like a cathedral in scale, enclosed on three sides by the downed ship and open to the plains to the west. The camp walls jutted from the ground well clear of the ship's exterior, the gates thrown wide open to reveal the distant distraction taking place far beyond the crater.

Hunched figures were briefly silhouetted by las-beams that lanced into them from one side, drawing thunderous gunfire from the orks themselves as they charged down the threat. The sounds of battle came a heartbeat after each volley and distant explosion, delayed by the distance that the xenos had already been drawn from the camp; there was no way to know what toll the fighting might be having on his troops, but the distraction appeared to be working.

But not all of the orks had taken the bait.

They moved about in the well-lit enclosure that they had carved from the ship and the earth, loping to and fro with a swinging gait, occasionally casting longing looks towards the gates and the fight they clearly wanted to join. A lumpen brute stood at the centre of their labours, directing their actions as a conductor might control an ill-disciplined orchestra.

'The magazine survived the crash,' Leontus breathed as he saw what the orks were sorting through – great brass shells the size of church bells were being rolled across the dirt to waiting trukks, whilst others carried long grey missiles over their sloping shoulders. Still more shovelled shoota rounds from crates into holed and torn sacks, spilling bullets to the floor in tinkling rain that no one paid any mind.

'This is how we destroy this place,' he said, and pointed to the shadowed corners of the chamber far from where the orks worked. 'You plant your charges there. We keep low and move quickly, in case–'

Something moved in the dark recesses where Leontus had indicated; a broad figure wearing a red bandanna crawled behind a stack of waiting shells, their lasgun cradled in their arms as they moved towards the end of a disordered stack.

A diminutive creature leaped from the shells with a shriek, its voice attracting the attention of the other xenos as it landed on the Catachan's back and stabbed wildly at his flesh with a short knife. The Catachan let out a roar of pain as he twisted and struck out at the grot, but his blows caught only air as it leaped aside. The creature paced sideways menacingly, readying itself for another leap, when the massive ork in the centre of the room made itself heard.

''Ere, wot's happenin' back dere?' it bellowed, its voice echoing across the high ceiling.

'We should–' Nomak began, but Leontus silenced him with a look. He knew Nomak did not understand the beast, nor would he see the value in doing so. For Leontus, learning to passably understand the ork tongue – however distasteful it was – had proven a valuable decision a dozen times over.

'They're on alert now,' he said. 'We wait.'

The ork stomped forward when no one replied, lifting a massive shoota as it made its way to where the grot still menaced the wounded Catachan.

'Dere's a 'umie 'ere!' the creature squealed, cackling at the Catachan's attempts to grab at it as it danced away.

The huge ork fired its weapon in a chuntering burst of flame and solid projectiles that mercifully missed the stacked ordnance in front of it. The rounds punched holes in the bulkhead above the Catachan, however, and sprayed both him and the grot with falling debris as the large ork laughed. The others it had been directing began laughing along with it – a low, forced rumble that was entirely foreign to the human equivalent.

'We should move while they're distracted,' Belgutei whispered, but Leontus shook his head.

Another ork stepped down from the cab of a waiting trukk in the swish of a dirty white coat, its limbs a motley collection of crude augmetics, hissing pistons, and a too-long arm that ended in a battered ceramite gauntlet that had no business being on an ork's wrist. Leontus couldn't guess where the xenos had stolen a Space Marine's narthecium gauntlet – the grisly tool of an Apothecary's craft, meant for field triage – but each blasphemous twitch and spasm of its dangling cutting blades turned his stomach.

He had seen far more altered orks in his career, but it wasn't the creature's limbs that drew his attention; it was its head. Long dreadlocks of rubber hose and segmented metallic cabling hung from its scalp and ears in a tangled mass, the flexible lengths dangling to its waist with the weight of what had been primitively stitched to their ends: ork heads, dangling by their spinal cords or by rough metal ports drilled through their scalps, or hung within misted glass jars that clinked and grated as the ork moved. Each grotesque decoration even blinked in time with its owner, their eyelids drooping in macabre imitation of life.

The newcomer walked up behind the large ork and jabbed it with a brass device held in an augmetic claw, and a sharp snap echoed through the chamber. The others stopped laughing immediately as their once-leader dropped to the floor in a dead heap, smoke rising lazily from its scorched skin.

'We don't use da shootas near da zoggin' bombs!' the dreadlocked ork roared, and Leontus' stomach turned as he saw the decorative heads mouthing along with the creature's words. 'How many times does we 'ave to say it?'

Leontus looked away from the grotesque creature to the lumen globes suspended from mismatched cabling in the ceiling, each connected in a long chain of cannibalised wires that led across to the other end of the chamber. They disappeared into a puttering box that looked as if it had been dragged from an industrial spoil yard, but was apparently some kind of promethium generator.

"Umie, we'z gonna ask you once to come out an' be done in quick,' the ork shouted. 'Uvverwise we'll do it slow an' painful like.'

'There's a promethium generator on the other side of the room. Can you hit it from here?' Leontus asked Belgutei.

The Attilan glanced over to where the machine stood pumping out black smoke, and nodded once.

'Good. Get in, plant your charges, and make for the gates. I will make a run for the Catachan.'

'What about Arnetz and her team?' Nomak hissed as Belgutei took aim.

'Set your charges to a ten-minute delay,' Leontus said. 'Shoot.'

A burst of las-bolts slammed into the generator in a tight grouping, eliciting a high-pitched whine from the machine. At once, the lights dimmed and died, plunging the scene into darkness.

'Dere's more dan one 'umie!' the grotesque ork shouted from the heart of the darkness. 'Find 'em and kill 'em!'

Leontus ran at a crouch to where he had last seen the Catachan, blindly navigating his way through the scattered shells until he heard a scratchy little voice crying out not in pain, but in victory.

He didn't understand the orkish words it was screeching, but he could guess at their meaning as a series of wet, gurgling gasps came from nearby – the grot had cut the Catachan's throat and was crowing over its kill. Leontus slowed; his attempt to reach the trooper was futile now, but he could still send the abhorrent little creature to meet its makers.

He ignited Conquest's power field. The sword's cold azure light reached a still form framed in a pool of dark blood, and the grot on the body looked up at him in sheer terror.

One swipe was all it took to bisect the xenos in a sizzle of gristle and stringy meat, and he deactivated the blade before its torso hit the ground.

'We saw dat!' the ork boss jeered, and it laughed. With

a teeth-grinding buzz of restrained lightning, the beast was bathed in sudden light, its augmetic claw raised and the brass weapon crackling in its grip. Spiderwebs of energy played across the metal limb, each fizzling away into nothing as they sank beneath its coat and into the flesh beneath.

Leontus stood and faced the creature, separated by a sea of scattered shells and haphazardly discarded munitions. The other orks watched on, looking to the half-mechanical abomination to give them leave to attack.

'You are the leader of this… mob?' Leontus asked. The Attilans couldn't have planted their charges and escaped in the few seconds before he'd been seen, but if he could keep the creature's attention on him…

'We are,' the creature said with a nod that set the dangling heads to rattling. Its eyes were wide and unblinking as it studied him, almost as if it recognised him. 'But we fink we know who you is. We'z seen ya before.'

'I don't believe that we've met.'

'Nah, we'z not met. But we knows you from da statues and da little movin' pictures,' it said with a widening smile. 'You'z Lee-on-at-us.'

'I am Lord Solar Leontus,' Leontus said, strangely intrigued at the creature's butchery of his name. 'But I don't know who you are.'

Confusion crossed the creature's face then, its eyes darting away as if it were trying to remember something important. Leontus tried to keep all of the other orks in his eyeline as the shadows danced across the walls, flickering as the unstable lightning in the ork's hand buzzed and curled.

'We'z Bad Doc Stitcha,' it said, and flexed the arm wearing the narthecium gauntlet. 'We'z Big Mek Gorbat, too.' It shook the arm holding the lightning weapon, then swung the captive heads in a showman's flourish. 'And we'z all da uvver 'ardest nobz as well.'

''E's da 'Ead Nobz,' one of the orks growled, as if it were information that Leontus shouldn't have had to ask.

The orks' recent cohesion made far more sense if they had been united beneath one banner, especially if that one banner encapsulated what looked like every faction for miles in every direction. The thought that the severed heads might somehow be feeding through into one unified being turned his stomach, despite knowing that ork depravity knew no bounds.

'There ain't been no good scraps for ages, before you krumped Irontoof,' the 'Ead Nobz said, a mischievous glimmer flashing in his eye. 'Izzat why dey gave you loadsa statues? Cos you'z proppa killy?'

'One of the reasons,' Leontus said. 'Several were for killing orks.'

'Ha! Yeah, you sounds up for a good scrap, like wot da Prophet got wiv Ol' Bale Eye.' The 'Ead Nobz gave a vigorous nod, which set the heads to swing by his sides. Leontus had no idea what he was talking about, but continued to play for time.

'You don't want me for an enemy,' Leontus said.

'We fink we does. You'z a finkin' scrapper, it's why you'z in 'ere instead of dyin' wiv your boyz out dere,' the 'Ead Nobz said with a fang-toothed approximation of a wide grin, waving the narthecium gauntlet towards the sounds of battle still raging outside the camp's walls. 'We tells you what, we'll let Gork an' Mork decide. We'z gonna head out and join da fight proppa, see how many of your boyz we can kill, an' how about you come find us wiv all da 'umies you 'ave? Den we'll have a proppa good scrap.'

The ork spoke the words as if he were impressed with

his own fairness, nodding to himself as he turned on his augmetic limbs and stomped back to the trukk with his lightning weapon held aloft. The light dimmed as he walked away, the mouths of the other orks widening in predatory smiles, until, with a final snap of discharged electricity, they were all plunged into darkness again.

'Get 'im!'

Arnetz launched herself through the bulkhead into the darkness beyond before the ork's shout had time to echo, her lasgun spitting shots that strobed through the open chamber and out into the night. She'd missed the back of the trukk as it tore out of the open gates, but the las-bolts at least illuminated the orks charging towards the Lord Solar.

Barratt's squad opened fire at the same moment over to her right. Two orks were spun from their feet as the las-bolts blasted scorched holes in their flesh.

'Hold your fire!' the Lord Solar roared, and suddenly he was in front of her, his teeth shining in the dark as he pushed the barrel of her lasgun into the air. 'Make for the gates, now!'

They ran together, the Catachans and the Lord Solar, the thumping of their boots and their dancing lumens a rallying call for the searching orks. Iron-shod footfalls rang out as the xenos gave chase, their ragged, harsh breathing giving away their location as much as their cries of surprise and pain when they stumbled over shells and strewn missiles.

Arnetz spotted Belgutei and the other Attilans as she ran, waving them on frantically as he and his men prepared to open fire. Someone cried out behind her as they were caught, their defiant screams lost beneath the animal roars of orks pouncing on their wounded prey.

'Turn and face!' Leontus shouted, and she slid to a stop on

the hard-packed soil and did as she was ordered alongside her squad; the orks were rushing forward in a crazed mob, their hands reaching out to claw and tear…

Lasguns crackled in desperate hands, snapping out shots on full-auto to scythe through the xenos like the vengeful hand of the God-Emperor. Arnetz tasted the tang of ozone on the air, her heartbeat hammering in her ears like a beating drum as Leontus stepped forward and added his pistol's fire to the fusillade, then met the last ork glowing blade to swinging axe.

She heard his grunt of effort as he parried the first blow, then swung Conquest in a tight arc to slice through both the ork's arms in a single swing, bringing the shimmering blade round in one fluid motion to hack through the beast's neck. His breathing matched hers as he heaved in lungfuls of air laced with the tang of las-fire and the orks' dank musk.

Arnetz turned at the sound of las-fire behind her, beyond the compound's open gates.

'My lord, we need to get out of here,' she said breathlessly.

'Are the charges planted?' he asked.

Belgutei nodded, and both Barratt and Arnetz made noises of assent.

'Then let's be clear of this place.'

Arnetz led the survivors away from the ship towards the hills at a run, not only to escape the orks who still fought the diversionary force but to get clear of the ship before it died its second death.

She felt the blast through her feet as a shock wave of heat washed over them all, followed almost instantaneously by a howl of mechanical pain. The aftershocks of the blast still shook the earth as metal screamed and twisted, and she looked back to see a fireball rising towards the heavens, collapsing in on itself to become a column of boiling smoke. The flames washed the plains in yellows and oranges, a false dawn that cast long shadows behind the dead scattered across the grass.

Leontus was the first to turn away, barking orders for them to move as the ship creaked and began to fall, its ancient bones given animus for the last time as it collapsed in on itself. Arnetz urged the others on, but each time she looked back, Leontus was watching the last gasps of the diversionary attack to the north, rather than the destruction they'd left in their wake.

ELEVEN

Belgutei was beyond exhaustion long before the night was through; to him, fatigue and weariness were but distant and pleasant memories. Each step was an ordeal, a catalogue of aches and stabbing pain where his blisters had worn through to the raw flesh beneath. The Catachans seemed immune to tiredness, apparently coasting along on their reserves of adrenaline and sheer bloody-mindedness, which the Attilans fought to match as their forced march rolled on.

Arnetz led them on a circuitous route through the foothills, up and down identical rises and across low valleys, twisting and turning back on themselves, until Csaba spoke up to ask if they were lost.

'She's masking our trail,' Belgutei told him through clenched teeth, pushing down on his knees in a vain attempt to make the latest climb easier. 'The orks know that we're here now. They will be looking for us by dawn.'

He heard the river before they saw it.

'I'll create false trails up into the hills with my squad,' Arnetz said. 'There's another couple of hours before dawn, which should be long enough for you to work your way upriver and back to the plateau near the cavern, my lord.'

'God-Emperor go with you, Arnetz,' Leontus said. In the half-light cast by the stars, it was difficult to make out much, but Belgutei saw the Lord Solar shake the Catachan's hand. Then he turned to the Attilans.

'Belgutei, you and your men are with me.'

At first, the cold water was like a salve to his aching and blistered feet, but the relief only lasted until he tried to move and found that they'd trebled in weight in the water. The Lord Solar seemed unaffected, and strode across the riverbed and up the rocky slopes like a steppes goat, much to Belgutei's annoyance.

The feeling gave him a moment's energy, which was enough to get him moving once more.

The Lord Solar was the first back into the slot canyon, and led Belgutei and the others through the claustrophobic darkness of the cavern to find fires already lit and surrounded by Cadians seeing to their weapons and gear.

Andersson stood as the Lord Solar entered, rising wearily to his feet and saluting as Belgutei collapsed onto his bedroll and let out a relieved sigh.

'Good work with the distraction. Did you get away cleanly?' the Lord Solar asked, and the Cadian murmured his assent.

'We did, for the most part. Raust's last attack pulled the worst of the orks off us to give us time to get away. I've been wandering the foothills most of the night to confuse any pursuers – we've been back less than an hour.'

'Losses?'

'Minimal. Raust's squads bore the brunt of it. We picked up a few of the stragglers from his command, but no great numbers.'

'Thank you, sergeant,' Leontus said, and made to step past the Cadian.

'My lord, if I may,' Andersson said, stopping the Lord Solar in his tracks. 'I'd like to put Sergeant Raust forward for a commendation, when this is all over.'

'Already done, sergeant. Carry on,' Leontus said. He unclasped his helm and slipped it under his arm as he walked to the first campfire and spoke to the Cadians sitting there, before moving on to the next.

'A commendation from a Cadian? Raust must have really impressed you,' Belgutei said as Andersson took his seat by the first fire, the flames giving the deep shadows under his eyes a bruise-like quality.

'It's the least I could do after tonight. It was a damned brave thing he did.'

'I'm sure he'll show you his best smile when he gets back,' Belgutei said with a grunted laugh, throwing an arm over his eyes in an attempt to block out the light.

'What are you talking about?'

'A smile,' Belgutei said with a sigh, propping himself up on one arm to face the Cadian's stare. 'You know, because of the mask. You can't see his face–'

'You know Raust isn't coming back, right?'

Belgutei's guts twisted.

'Oh God-Emperor,' Belgutei said, holding up a hand in apology. 'I didn't know, I… Did you see him fall?'

'Of course not.' Andersson shook his head and turned back to the fire. 'That was the point.'

'Now you've lost me,' Belgutei said as the Cadian glanced to where the Lord Solar now knelt on the upper level.

'Raust's orders. You understood what he volunteered for?' Andersson asked in a low voice. 'He led the rearguard once we'd pulled the orks away from the ship. He sacrificed himself and his men to occupy the xenos long enough for us to escape.'

Belgutei stared as Andersson turned with a sigh, the man's black mood suddenly more than understandable. He pushed himself to his feet, his earlier fatigue burned away by his rising anger as he moved through the Cadians and their fires. He half-ran up the slope that led to the Lord Solar, ignoring Andersson's shouts to come back.

'You ordered Raust to sacrifice himself and his men?' Belgutei spat.

The Lord Solar turned from where he knelt by the river, stripped to the waist as he rubbed the camo-paint from his breastplate and helm. His bare torso was an abstract tapestry of surgical scars and long-healed wounds, with the addition of a fresh gash on his forearm that bled freely down his wrist. He looked smaller without his armour, less like an avenging hero and more like the mere mortal he was.

'He volunteered, but yes, I gave the order,' the Lord Solar said. 'It was a necessary part of the plan, and maximised–'

'You ordered a man to his death. You ordered him to lead his men to their deaths. I did not think that you–'

'I have done it before and will again if it is required,' the Lord Solar said, pushing himself to his feet. 'Do not misunderstand me, sergeant – as I have already told you, I feel the weight of each of those decisions and will until my dying day.'

Belgutei ignored the Lord Solar's use of his rank rather than his name, and the subtle reproach that the word carried with it.

'Yesterday you said that I should not want their deaths on my soul,' Belgutei said, pointing to the soldiers gathered on the level below. 'But without hesitation, you sent so many to their deaths?'

'I did,' the Lord Solar said. 'I sent us all to a probable death last night. If less than half of us had returned, I would still have considered it a victory.'

'Our lives are just currency for you to pay the price of victory?'

'Of course they are!' the Lord Solar snapped, muscles tensing along his jawline as he glared at Belgutei. 'My life, your life, the lives of everyone here – they are the bulwark against the darkness. On Fortuna Minor it is the xenos. On the next world it may be the mutant, or the heretic. We will fight until we can fight no longer, and pass our weapons to those that may continue the fight. That is the way of the Astra Militarum.'

Belgutei was aware of many eyes on him, and looked down to see the Cadians looking up at the exchange from their campfires, but the Lord Solar didn't relent. He stepped in close, his voice a dangerous whisper.

'Raust understood the bigger picture – what we needed to achieve and what was required to give us the best chance of success. He volunteered to take command of the wounded and the sick, and give their deaths a purpose. That is all that any of us can hope for in the end.'

'I did not think you were that kind of leader,' Belgutei said.

'I am the leader that the Imperium requires,' the Lord Solar said, stepping back as the anger left his expression to be replaced by a bone-deep fatigue. 'You do not mourn Raust, Belgutei. You mourn an idea of what I might be for you and the others, not what we lost tonight.'

'Do not tell me what–'

'Where did he win his first medal for bravery?' the Lord Solar asked, but Belgutei found that he had no reply to give. He hadn't spoken to the Krieg man at any length outside of battle, let alone consider that there was much to talk to behind his blank-eyed respirator.

The Lord Solar did not relent. 'It was for valorous conduct on Rosenghast III. Did he tell you of the first time he met the enemies of mankind in battle? Or the sermons of Saint Gerstahl that he had memorised to recite to his troops when faced with true horror?'

Belgutei wanted to turn away, to look at something other than the Lord Solar as he was shamed for his short-sightedness. The man's eyes held him in place with their cold intensity, their warmth replaced by a void from which there was no release.

'There is a proverb on Attila,' Belgutei said when he finally found the strength to speak. 'We say that over a shared lifetime, a rider and their mount will become one beast, inseparable and indistinguishable from one another. I see that is true of you and the machine you call a horse – there is more servo than soul left in either of you.'

The Lord Solar said nothing for a few moments, letting the sound of the river fill the space where silence should have been.

'Go and rest, sergeant. Somewhere that I can see you,' he said at last. Belgutei saluted and made for the lower level, ignoring the Cadians' cold stares as he wound his way through their campfires to the Attilans' corner of the cave.

Nomak was waiting for him, his expression unreadable. He found his voice as Belgutei dropped onto his bedroll.

'What the hell was that about?'

'A misunderstanding,' Belgutei said.

* * *

Arnetz slipped back into the cavern with her squad just in time to see Belgutei take to his bedroll, watched by everyone else gathered around the small campfires dotted around the lower level. Tension hung heavy in the air, like the mists already forming over the lake beyond the canyon, only fuelled by the furtive glances being passed between the Cadians. Whilst she hadn't expected them to be wildly celebrating the mission's success, she also hadn't expected to be returning to a tinderbox awaiting the igniting spark.

Andersson raised his hand in greeting, then waved her over to him, the old Cadian's grim face confirming that something wasn't right with the attack's survivors.

'Belgutei and the Lord Solar are at loggerheads,' he muttered under the pretence of handing her a canteen of clean water. 'I couldn't hear it all, but it wasn't good.'

She took a long drink and passed the canteen back with a nod of thanks. 'What did you hear?'

'They mentioned Raust,' he said with a reflexive glance to the corner that housed their meagre stores. 'The Lord Solar reminded him of our duty to the Imperium.'

Arnetz let out a sigh. She was beyond tired; adrenaline had fuelled their fight through Ultima and she'd ridden the fumes of that energy in the escape, but after hours of climbing and doubling back, obscuring tracks and misdirections, she needed a few hours of undisturbed sleep. It seemed that was still just out of her reach.

'The Lord Solar's bleeding,' she said, pointing up to where Leontus scrubbed at his armour, seemingly ignoring the streak of dark blood running down his forearm. 'I'll see if I can smooth it out.'

Her men joined the Cadians around their fires, sharing canteens and rations as they talked of anything and everything except the night's events, whilst Arnetz collected the last of her medicae supplies and made her way to the Lord Solar's perch. She found him still by the riverside, a scrap of dirty cloth in one hand and his breastplate across his knees.

'Lord Solar,' she said with a salute. 'I've come to look at your arm, my lord.'

'What? No, it can wait,' he said with a dismissive wave of his hand, only briefly glancing at the open wound on his arm. 'Sergeant Andersson has several wounded who are in far greater need of your attention.'

'With respect, my lord, I need to close it to prevent infection.'

She drew her surgical stapler as she approached the Lord Solar, dropping to one knee beside him to examine the torn flesh. It was deep and bleeding freely, the skin parting to reveal a metallic twist of bloodstained silver – an augmetic enhancement, bonded to the muscle fibres of his arm. He relented as she began to wipe the dirt and congealed blood from the edges of the wound, and held it closed as she applied the staples with three sharp cracks. On the fourth, the mechanism clicked empty, the last of her good medicae supplies spent. She would have to move on to improvised alternatives, or else propose a scavenging mission to the fields at Bruke.

'Thank you, sergeant,' the Lord Solar said. 'For this, and for your actions in Ultima. You likely saved my life.'

She smiled and shook her head, weighing the surgical stapler in her hand. It was empty, its resources spent and used up. Every instinct told her to discard it, to shed the extra weight, but she slipped it back into her pack. Perhaps she was becoming sentimental, she thought.

'Permission to speak freely, my lord?'

'At least you have the grace to ask,' the Lord Solar said. He laughed mirthlessly, but didn't stop her.

'The orks in Ultima weren't just collecting guns and munitions. They were scavenging hull plating, circuitry, hydraulic servos...'

'And cabling,' the Lord Solar added.

'That too. I'm not sure how all that was relevant to them fortifying the space port.'

The Lord Solar fixed her with a tired look and let out a long, slow breath. He turned his gaze to the gathered soldiery below, who ate and drank in a tempered celebration of their victory.

'Do you know what they're doing with all that materiel, my lord?' she pressed.

'I have my suspicions, and plans to counteract them should they be proven true,' he said. 'For now, you should rejoin the others below. Tomorrow we must begin planning for our attack on the space port.'

TWELVE

Teryn wasn't a coward.

She'd passed through the youth soldier programmes on Cadia with honours, fought her way through her Whiteshield posting, and even managed to win a medal for valour once. That was a few years ago, and she'd traded it to a Valhallan for a thick blanket and half a bottle of amasec almost immediately afterward. In the twenty years she'd spent as a fully fledged member of the Cadian Shock Troops, she'd never run from a fight once; before this world she'd been a hardened veteran, someone who the new recruits had looked up to with their wrong-coloured eyes.

That had changed on Fortuna Minor. The orks had chewed up the soldier that Teryn had been and spat out a trembling, fearful wreck, a shadow of the proud Cadian she was before.

Teryn wasn't a coward, but her lasgun still shook in her hands as the ork convoy approached. A nervous twitch started below her right eye, washing her vision with sudden tears as she tried to focus on the green-skinned monsters hanging from the sides of the lead vehicle.

'Steady now, steady. Wait for the Lord Solar's signal,' Andersson said from the long grass to her left, his words a scant reassurance as her limbs begged her to flee.

The orks had multiplied since the attack on their downed ship, seemingly drawn in from across the continent by the lure of a good scrap against the humans who'd finally revealed themselves. Either that or they'd seen the miles-high column of smoke that the Lord Solar had left in his wake, and had decided that there was more to do near the space port. It didn't matter to Teryn; all it meant was that there were far too many xenos in the region for her to sleep soundly any more.

Bikers mounted the bridge over the river, their tracks spitting sparks from the sheet metal surface as they sped over and back to the dirt track beyond. Behind them came the trukks and the strange armoured buggies the red-daubed xenos seemed to favour, brutish orks manning pintle-mounted heavy weapons of exotic and dubious design. The largest trukk bounced as it rumbled onto the bridge, the orks crammed into the flatbed shouting abuse at the driver that was cut short by a deafening boom.

The charges beneath the bridge sent the trukk flipping through the air, shedding tyres, thick plating, and eviscerated ork flesh as it spun down, lost in the dust kicked up by the shock wave.

'Now!' Andersson roared, his lasgun spitting death as he rose from the long grass. Lances of light whipped out from all directions, flashing what felt like inches away from Teryn's head as the ambushers pounced, secondary explosions and roaring engines competing for dominance in her mind.

Teryn did not join the others. She stayed on her knees in the grass and prayed to the God-Emperor for His protection.

The orks were far better prepared than Arnetz had expected, but they still fell to the hail of gunfire that she and the other squad leaders directed at the most dangerous threats.

Three trukks had made it over the bridge alongside the majority of their escort, a handful of bikes and buggies that swarmed around the larger vehicles like angry insects protecting their hive. A smaller transport had been isolated on the other side of the river, but that wasn't her immediate concern.

'Gunner on the lead buggy, take him down!' she roared, her lasgun growing hot in her hands as she sprayed a volley of shots at the orks vaulting from the lead trukk. Her squad obeyed, and the gunner dropped from the speeding buggy to tumble bonelessly in the dirt. His driver carried on at breakneck speed until a stray shot blew out one of its tyres, flipping the vehicle in a drumroll of crumpled metal.

'They're pushing from the east!' someone shouted, and Arnetz took one more shot at the leaping orks before looking over towards the bridge, where yet more xenos wearing blue-painted metal plating were trying to ford the river to get at their attackers.

'Barratt, push east with your squad and slow the reinforcements!' she shouted, and Barratt led his men from cover a moment later. They were Cadians for the most part, but they kept pace with their Catachan sergeant as they repositioned.

Arnetz's attention was drawn to the north, where one of the orks' bare-framed groundcars had ploughed into another of the Cadian concealed positions. Human forms tumbled through the air as it forced a path through grass and flesh alike in a macabre charge, its driver cackling madly as its wheels ground the beast's victims into the dirt.

'Damn fools should have moved,' she hissed. The position had been assigned to one of the new squads formed from liberated prisoners, but it didn't make the sight any easier to bear. 'Take that thing down!'

She fired at the open-sided groundcar and her squad followed her lead, arresting the vehicle's massacre as the beast driving it slumped behind the wheel, its body shot through with half a dozen las-bolts.

'I need support over here!'

Arnetz leaped to her feet without a second thought, sprinting across the ambush towards where Barratt and his squad were pumping bolt after bolt into the orks fording the river. They were slowed by the rushing water as it foamed about their waists, but were heavily armoured enough that they could wade through both the current and the hail of las-bolts raining down upon them.

'Bring them down!' Arnetz cried, aiming her shots at the exposed flesh between the orks' hammered plates. Her squad joined her, pouring volleys of scorching las into the xenos. The orks didn't turn away, however; they redoubled their efforts to reach the humans despite the weight of fire, falling one by one into the swell until the last one slipped beneath the surface in a cloud of dark blood. Their limp forms were dragged to the bottom of the river by the weight of their armour, tumbling against the stones as the current dragged them away.

The sounds of battle had faded away to nothing before she called the ceasefire, the last armoured ork's feeble crawl ending in the reeds of the opposite bank as a lucky las-beam blew out the back of its skull.

Dead xenos lay bleeding across the dirt road and grassy verges to either side of it, but they weren't the only casualties of the ambush. Several Cadians had fallen to ork shooting and the savage speed of their vehicles; nothing could be done to save the victims of either, even if Arnetz had still had any useful medicae supplies.

'Check the bodies,' she ordered as they made their way back towards the heart of the ambush. They knew to use their knives for the grim task of ensuring each of the xenos was dead, conserving ammunition by drawing serrated blades across throats or ramming them through eye sockets. She was the only Catachan with her own combat knife; the others carried long, serrated knives that had begun their service in the hands of the orks, their own Catachan blades lost when they were captured. It had become something of a rite of passage to replace them with the best knives that they could scavenge, even if the quality was incomparable.

'Three trukks, four smaller vehicles and three bikes,' Andersson said as Arnetz approached, a cut on his scalp plastering his hair to his head in a blackened smear. 'Not a bad day's hunting.'

'I can see why the Lord Solar had us wait for a bigger convoy. It would have been a shame to waste the bridge ambush on one of the scouting parties,' Arnetz said approvingly.

Andersson nodded to the north. 'Speaking of…'

The Lord Solar descended the incline and rode towards them, Belgutei following in his wake as if pulled on by an invisible leash; the Lord Solar hadn't let the Attilan out of his sight since their discussion following the destruction of Ultima, and Arnetz couldn't decide which was worse – Belgutei's simmering anger or his uninterested placidity.

'You're right, my lord. It looks like they've started moving troops instead of materiel,' Andersson called as the Lord Solar approached. It was strange to see the contrast in the way that Konstantin stood so still at his rider's most subtle command, where the Attilans' horses stomped and chafed as they were drawn up.

'We have denied them this cohort at least,' the Lord Solar said, though he didn't look to be pleased by their day's work.

'That's something,' Arnetz said. 'With your permission, I'd like to take my squad to the west to scout the new camps that have sprung up north of the space port. We've also identified a location in the foothills that might be suitable for another weapons cache, or even another staging area.'

'I'll take the foothills with Belgutei and his riders,' the Lord Solar said. His gaze had shifted skyward, a habit that she had noticed in him in the days since the destruction of Ultima.

The orks were aware of them now, that the ambushes and night attacks weren't merely warring clans but an external threat that had managed to stay hidden until the last possible moment. More orks had been drawn to the area, increasing security around their convoys and honest-to-goodness patrols – a knowledge of tactical procedure that she would never have thought the orks capable of.

But the Lord Solar hadn't been idle; they had learned that the orks were uniting under the freakish creature that the orks called the 'Ead Nobz, and his tactics had changed accordingly. They were more selective with their ambushes, saving their resources for only the most valuable targets whilst increasing their own numbers in raids on ork encampments that showed any sign of captive humans. As a result, they had outgrown the cavern on the plateau, and several smaller bases had been set up in the labyrinthine foothills to house and hide their movements in the night. Several caches had been established too, to spread their meagre resources beyond their main base of operations, but they were still hopelessly outnumbered and outgunned by the orks even before more xenos began migrating to the area.

'The skies look clear for now,' Arnetz said, following the natural impulse to look where another person did. The skies were clear of clouds and the dark specks of aircraft – just a wash of deep blue that brightened to near-white as it met the horizon.

'Leave some scouts here to watch for ork activity around the bridge – they may try to repair it,' the Lord Solar said, twitching the reins in his hand so Konstantin turned away to the west. 'I will see you back at the cavern after nightfall.'

'As you command, my lord,' Arnetz said, both she and Andersson making the sign of the aquila as the Lord Solar rode off. The infantry would head north by squad, back along the circuitous paths they'd taken to descend through the foot-hills, according to the Lord Solar's orders to minimise the chances of detection.

'I'll stay with a few of my people,' Andersson said. 'I hope you find something that helps lift the mood.'

'You just want us to find something good to eat,' Arnetz said with a smile.

Andersson laughed. 'I'd take that.'

'A lucky one for you. I'll see what we find on the way,' Arnetz said. 'Catachans, form up! The rest of you fall back by squads to the cavern or your forward bases.'

She left Andersson as he selected a few members of his squad to remain behind; he chose two young men with auburn hair and a pale-faced woman who looked like she hadn't slept properly in weeks.

* * *

Belgutei rode behind the Lord Solar with Nomak by his side, Rugen and Csaba bringing up the rear with their lasguns primed and ready. There was no conversation as they went, no jokes or jibes at one another's expense. Their attention was focused on the land around them and the sky above, watching for any sign that they might come under attack as they headed further to the west.

Despite what the Lord Solar had said to Arnetz about scouting a possible cache site, Belgutei knew where they were going first. The Lord Solar was leading them towards the space port to scout the perimeter again, just as he did at every opportunity, his obsession with the ork-held structure becoming addiction-like in his need to understand every point of ingress, every strongpoint and weakness, the number of orks on guard at different times of day, and the numbers that came and went with each convoy.

All that Belgutei could see was an impenetrable fortress that had grown up around the Imperial buildings like a fungus leeching nutrients from rotting wood. Two guard towers had been erected seemingly overnight, one either side of the gargantuan gates that were the only visible access to the hangars and spire within. The walls grew higher and higher with each viewing, the badly welded plating swaying in the wind as ill-fitted rivets fell like rain, each foot of height accompanied by a visible strain on the panels beneath. A small mountain of scrap had been piled up around the spire's base as they apparently tried to reinforce it or build a ship around its foundations. Belgutei had long since given up trying to understand the workings of the xenos' minds; there was no way that heap of welded pig-iron would fly, even if they turned the high walls into flapping wings.

Had they possessed any heavy armour or long-range ordnance, then they would likely have been able to break through the walls with little effort, but they didn't. All they had was a heavy bolter with next to no ammunition and a temperamental autocannon with even fewer shells than the heavy bolter. Even Belgutei and his riders were down to their last few melta lances, though they'd managed to fashion a few working krak-tipped hunting lances. What they did have was a growing number of mouths to feed and an excess of lasguns, neither of which was going to get them inside the walls.

He understood the Lord Solar's obsession for what it was: desperation. They had finally come up against an obstacle that he could not out-plan or outmanoeuvre. Clever tactics wouldn't break them through the gates or the fortress walls, no matter how many times they scouted the perimeter.

The tip of the space port's spire came into view ahead, two dark shapes just visible in the sky beyond, and the Lord Solar called a halt. He still used Do-Song's magnoculars, which Belgutei supposed were more the Lord Solar's now than the dead Attilan's. He didn't draw his own battered pair; he didn't need to see the same thing he'd seen the last three times.

They could not breach the walls from the outside. And even if there were still ships inside that they could steal to get them back into orbit, there was little chance of reaching them through the hundreds of orks in the fortress.

'Spread out and keep an eye on our approach,' Belgutei said, and the other riders nudged their horses into better positions. Whilst he'd never known orks to deploy scouting parties outside their camps before Fortuna Minor, the sign of their passage became more evident with each recce of the space port. They were ranging further from their fortress each time, something that the Lord Solar had remarked upon too.

'If I may ask, my lord,' Belgutei said after a few minutes, 'what exactly is it you are looking for?'

He kept his tone neutral but not warm; there had been no warmth between himself and the Lord Solar since Ultima, when Leontus had shown himself to be the politician that Belgutei had always thought he was.

'A mistake,' the Lord Solar said without lowering his magnoculars, 'and to see if they have the wit to repair it before we exploit it.'

'I do not see anything.'

'That's because you have no imagination, Belgutei. There are a handful of ways inside that fortress. We only need one.'

Belgutei bit back a venomous retort. Imagination wouldn't open the gates of that fortress; as far as he could see, only the orks could do that.

Teryn bit at her nails, wincing as she caught the soft skin of the nail bed again. She tasted copper, and spat the hard lump into the long grass as her finger began to throb.

They were high on a hillside overlooking the ambush site, four Cadians against whatever rolled down the dirt road towards them. The bulk of the Lord Solar's pitiful little army had marched away to the north hours ago, and she sorely wished that she'd been with them instead of stuck waiting for the orks to find them.

It was Andersson's fault. He'd chosen her because he knew she hadn't fired a shot during the ambush. It was punishment for keeping her head down when the bullets started flying, for hiding in the grass when the orks had charged from their trukks and driven their bastardised groundcars into Larrat's squad. He thought she was a coward, but she wasn't that. She couldn't be that.

'I'm seeing some movement to the east,' one of the others muttered from over to her left. 'Looks like vehicles...'

'And the south, this side of the riverbank,' Andersson said from her right.

Teryn couldn't see anything but the grass beneath her. Her limbs wouldn't obey her; she couldn't even raise her head. It was all she could do to try and breathe through the fearful hammering of her heart.

'Teryn, do you see anything? Teryn?'

She ignored Andersson, even as she heard him move through the grass. He was trying to keep quiet, but his boots sounded heavy as the dead grass crunched beneath each step.

'Teryn, what are you– Gah!'

Lasguns snapped wildly as someone screamed, their cries of alarm cut short with sudden wet crunches that she remembered from her nightmares. Adrenaline surged through her and she scrambled to her feet, coming face to face with an ork wearing a barbaric imitation of camouflage, a knitted hat perched on its head as it looked at her in surprise. It gripped a bloody axe in one hand, and an auburn-haired head in the other.

Teryn ran, dropping her lasgun as the screaming finally stopped.

THIRTEEN

'Should we wait for Andersson before we start, my lord?'

'No. I don't expect him back for a while yet.'

The Lord Solar had long since scrubbed the etchings of Tertius, Secundus, and Ultima from the rear wall of the cavern and replaced them with a plan of the space port, complete with scrawled lettering that denoted each structure and its assumed purpose. The standard layout pattern had been inscribed using a pale grey river stone, with the orks' additions marked with the dark orange of a rusted buckle.

Arnetz watched as he added yet more notes to the drawing with the stone, scratching out estimated heights and increasing the numbers in minor increments.

'I've identified another possible weakness. The northern wall still looks like the likeliest candidate for collapse,' the Lord Solar said as he stepped back. 'A strong southerly wind should do it, provided that they don't reinforce the upper layers before then.'

'Any plan that relies on a heavy dose of luck isn't exactly a reliable plan, my lord,' Arnetz said with a wince.

'No, it's not,' he agreed. 'But we'd be negligent not to note a possible opportunity.'

'I still think there might be some merit to the plan you mentioned before – the Trojan Equus?'

'It's not workable. Too many variables at play, not to mention getting one of their vehicles to work.'

Arnetz's attention turned from their rudimentary map to the Lord Solar, to the focus written clearly across his features. Greying stubble was beginning to show across his jawline and cheeks, ageing him more than the curls of silver hair he had taken to hiding beneath the Radiant Helm in front of the troops.

'We will find a way in, my lord. We just need more time.'

'I already have a way in,' the Lord Solar said.

Arnetz blinked in surprise at the admission. 'You do, my lord?'

'The path of greatest resistance, so to speak,' he said. 'What did you find in the new camp to the north-west?'

'We couldn't get too close in daylight, but there's some workable information that we can act on.'

'Such as?'

'The orks weren't present in any great numbers, I'd say twenty of them at the most. They appear to be dragging a great deal of construction materials south towards the space port – at their current pace, no more than a couple of days away.'

The Lord Solar nodded, his attention still focused on the space port plan.

'Did you say dragging?' he asked after a few moments.

'I did, my lord,' Arnetz said. She glanced towards the cavern floor, where Belgutei and his riders were playing cards in their corner.

'What is it?'

'Horses, my lord. They were using horses to drag the materials.'

The Lord Solar's expression hardened as he considered her words. She couldn't tell if the information had surprised him as it had her once she'd recognised the beasts toiling beneath the orks' cruel treatment.

'Any sign of Attilans?' he asked.

'Not from our position. We could go back tonight and try to get closer?'

'No, not tonight. We need to consider our options before we make our next move. That will be all, Arnetz.'

She saluted and made for the slope down to the lower level, but the Lord Solar called her back.

'Sergeant, one more thing,' he said, his voice dropping to a soft murmur. 'I think it would be best if you and your team kept this information from the others, at least for now.'

Arnetz looked over to where Belgutei sat laughing with his men; she knew exactly who the Lord Solar meant by 'others' in that instance.

'Of course, my lord.'

The Lord Solar dismissed her with a nod and turned back to the space port's etching on the wall.

She was still considering Belgutei and the thorny problem of the space port when Barratt called her over to a campfire ringed by the other Catachans and their adopted Cadians.

'Any news from the Lord Solar?' he asked as she took her seat and accepted a skewer of that afternoon's catch.

'Nothing to report yet,' she said. She checked the heat of the meat with her hands before biting into it; the last thing the encampment needed was an outbreak of food poisoning. 'Who's on sentry duty tonight?'

'A couple of Andersson's squad. We're not taking over until after midnight.'

She looked at the faces around the fires as she chewed, scanning the room in case Andersson had returned whilst she was with the Lord Solar, but he was still nowhere to be seen.

'What do you think, sarge?' one of the Cadians asked, holding up his own skewer of greasy meat.

'Needs salt. A lot of salt,' she said with a tired smile.

Teryn's throat and lungs burned with each ragged inhalation, each running step sending shockwaves of pain through her legs as she thudded up the last slope and out onto the plateau.

She'd been running for hours without stopping; the beasts were right behind her, she could feel it. She could hear their laughter each time she cast a fearful look over her shoulder, the sound of their heavy footfalls mixing with the echoes of her own as she'd dashed through narrow canyons towards safety, towards salvation.

Her breaths emerged as steaming plumes as she continued her stumbling sprint through the dark, skirting the lakeside on her route north towards the cavern. Dark shapes glittered in the water's depths, her mind conjuring red-eyed devils that were only a few steps behind her, even if they disappeared each time she turned.

The others would understand. They had been ambushed by orks. It wasn't her fault.

Her toes slammed into a solid obstacle in the dark, a rock or grassy protuberance that sent her tumbling down the lake bank with a hiss of pain. Rocks scraped the skin from her hands and elbows, tearing at the fabric of her trousers as she skidded to a halt and tried to scramble onwards on her hands and knees.

They would catch her now. She'd fallen at the last hurdle, and they would punish her...

But no blow came, no sudden pain in her shoulder blades or blazing agony in the base of her skull. She slowed her desperate sprint and allowed her mind to process the last few hours. There had been no laughter. The footsteps she'd heard were her own, echoing back to her from the stone-walled canyons. She'd likely left the orks behind before the sun went down; they'd be wandering the hillsides even now, searching for her long after she'd made good her escape.

The slot canyon was ahead of her, less than two hundred yards away, the high walls just visible in the light of the twin moons reflected from the surface of the river. Safety was within reach.

A heavy hand clamped over her mouth, stifling her desperate scream as boots crunched on the loose stones of the lake shore. Dark, hunched shapes strode past her without a second glance as she struggled against the hand that held her still. She scratched and bit at it, the horror of the cages consuming her conscious mind so that it was almost a relief when the blade sawed across her throat. The hand released her now that she was unable to scream, letting her fall to the floor as she tried to stem the flow of blood gouting from her open neck.

The last thing that Teryn saw was a pair of red eyes looking down at her in the darkness, and shooting stars blazing through the starry sky beyond.

'Subtle knife,' Belgutei said, throwing down a trio of worn playing cards onto a small pile of polished river stones.

'Lance,' Csaba said, and threw his cards down in disgust.

'Sword,' Rugen said through his mangled lips.

'Honour duel.' Nomak smiled, revealing his cards with a flourish.

'Bastard,' Belgutei grunted.

'I win again,' Nomak said, showing all of his teeth in his most punchable smile. He scooped up the tiny pile of stones, which they used as wagering chips, and added them to his pile, already double the size of anyone else's. Belgutei gathered the worn cards and started to shuffle them again, looking daggers at his second-in-command as he riffled them into a neat stack.

'Three times. Three fragging–'

Someone screamed a warning at the same moment the cavern boomed like a rung bell, an overload of sudden sound slapping at Belgutei's ears like a physical blow. Something wet and hot splashed his face as chips of stone sprayed down over his head, a hundred tiny pinpricks that saw him ducking aside on reflex alone.

His sword was in his hand as he pushed himself to his feet, debris still falling in a clattering rain that pattered off his armoured coat. He recognised the sound of the blast, even if his hearing had been reduced to a distant hum – it had been a grenade.

He numbly registered Nomak's prone form, face down on the cold stone where only moments before he had been laughing, blood staining his back and pouring from his broken skull.

Orks appeared in the cave mouth, stooped and howling with delight as they fired aimlessly into the defenceless humans arrayed before them. Belgutei pushed past Cadians as they scrambled for their weapons, vaulting a blackened corpse to be the first to meet the intruders blade to blade.

Do-Song's sword sang in his hand as the power field engaged, slicing the first ork's pistol in half as the creature raised it to fire; they were daubed in clumsy stripes, their green skin darkened by a black paste that covered flesh, weaponry, and clothing alike. Belgutei swayed away from the ork's return swing and barged forward, pushing the brute off balance as his blade deflected an axe that would have cleaved his head in two.

Then the Lord Solar was by his side, ploughing into the orks like a hurricane of sky blue and gold, Conquest licking out to end the xenos in brutal strikes, Sol's Righteous Gaze blasting bloody holes in the flesh of those he couldn't reach.

'To me, warriors of the God-Emperor! To me!' he roared.

The Lord Solar's voice broke the dam of silence in Belgutei's ears, unleashing a wall of sounds that battled for dominance: the blood-curdling wails of the wounded punctuated by the whip-crack report of lasguns, the roaring boom of the orks' solid-shot gunfire and the lightning snap of the Lord Solar's refractor field turning rounds aside.

But the battle cries of a dozen human throats overcame them all.

Bayonets and long knives struck out at the orks where he couldn't, bearing the green brutes down and finishing them with brutal blows as the Lord Solar shouted for someone to form a firing line.

Belgutei saw the old man through the corner of his eye, swaying aside from heavy blows only to strike back in a blur of gold and azure light, blood spraying with each swing of his sword.

'Belgutei, get the Lord Solar out of there!' a voice cried from behind.

He twisted away from a wild slash from a serrated blade, grabbing the Lord Solar's collar to drag him out of the fray and into the cavern. The Lord Solar glanced back once, Conquest rising for a piercing strike until he realised who had grabbed him, only then allowing himself to be steered away from the enemy.

A volley of las-bolts lanced past the moment Belgutei had

cleared the line of fire. The Lord Solar shrugged free from his grip and gave the order to fire again, and was obeyed by bleeding Catachans and scorched Cadians alike. Orks screamed as they fell, tumbling back from the cave mouth and out of sight, but the Lord Solar didn't relent.

'Are you hurt?' Arnetz shouted from her position beside the firing line. Belgutei's hand drifted up to his face, to the splattering of blood on his forehead and cheeks.

'It is not mine,' he replied, brushing the chips of stone from his hair. He cast about for any sign of his riders, but they were nowhere to be seen in the press of the fighting and the wounded.

The Lord Solar pushed his gunline forward, chasing the orks from the cave mouth and into the slot canyon. Belgutei followed, scooping up a Krieg-pattern lasgun as he ran to support the counter-attack.

The remaining orks turned and fled, chased through the canyon by bursts of las-fire that sprayed them with stone dust and chunks of lichen. The Lord Solar only called a halt to the pursuit when he reached the mouth of the slot canyon, breathing heavily as the few remaining orks were swallowed up by the void-black darkness of the plateau.

Belgutei knelt by the side of a dead sentry, the young Cadian's throat sliced almost to the bone, his blood black on the canyon walls in the moonlight. 'I will take my men, ride them down before they can report our position,' he said, barely able to hear his own voice beneath the ringing in his ears.

The Lord Solar shook his head. 'No, it's too late for that.' He still had Sol's Righteous Gaze in his hands, the muzzle glowing in the night air as he looked up into the starry sky.

'Then we must ride north, abandon the space port and–'

'We won't be forced into a rash decision by one band of

orks,' the Lord Solar said. 'The cavern has been compromised, so we disperse to the forward camps lower in the hills to consider our next move.'

'My lord–' Arnetz began as the Lord Solar made for the cavern, but he held up a hand to silence her.

'You have your orders. Gather the troops and make for the forward bases. Tonight,' he said as he stalked back down the canyon towards the cavern.

Arnetz watched him go, her mouth still open as if she still wanted to speak. Belgutei turned back towards the lake, taking in the glimmering reflections of the stars across the water. Some even moved, trailing fire as they burned a path across the heavens.

Do-Song had once told him that a falling star was an auspicious omen, that great things would come to those who saw them. As he turned back towards the cavern with Arnetz, he hoped that the dead man's words might be true.

FOURTEEN

Leontus scrubbed the outline of the space port from the wall with a damp rag, more from force of habit than out of any fear that the orks might divine his plans.

That the orks' attack had caught them by surprise could mean only one thing: they had been far too complacent with their main hideout, too sure in their ability to effectively defend such an isolated position. The enemy had punished that complacency, and in doing so had robbed him of more than just shelter – they had taken away access to a clean water source and forced him out into the open.

Worst of all, the orks had taken control of the war from him.

Someone cried out in pain from the cavern floor. He looked down to see Arnetz setting a man's arm with an improvised splint fashioned from a length of scavenged metal, the bandages little more than torn scraps of clothing. Her resourcefulness had limits, however; he didn't envy the way she had been forced to prioritise the wounded and the dying as they'd returned to the cavern.

Nor did he envy Belgutei.

The Attilans were gathered around Nomak, his still form pale even in the firelight. He'd apparently been caught by the initial volley of grenades rather than the fighting that followed, and his death would almost certainly hit Belgutei hard. The Attilan sergeant was kneeling next to the rider's body, speaking quiet words as he wiped blood and dirt from the dead man's face with a tender hand.

Several Cadians and two Catachans were similarly laid out nearby, watched over by their cold-eyed comrades as words were said to speed their souls to the God-Emperor's side.

'Arnetz, send messengers to the other camps,' he said as he descended the slope, Conquest in one hand and the Radiant Helm in the other. 'Tell them what happened and that our forces will be split between them until we find a new base of operations.'

Arnetz nodded. 'Yes, my lord.'

'Tell them to check their caches too, we might need the stored ammunition before long. Everyone else – get ready to move out.'

Leontus led his forces away from the cave and across the plateau in darkness, with Belgutei riding silently beside him. His eyes searched for any sign of the orks that had attacked the cavern, flicking occasionally to the low light twinkling across the lake's placid surface.

'I'm sorry about Nomak,' he said at last. 'He was a good man.'

'He was. We will miss his lance in the battles to come.'

'More than that, I think,' Leontus said. 'You knew him well?'

'He was my cousin. We grew up together on Attila, broke lances together in the hunting lodges… I will miss him.'

'There is an ancient saying on Terra,' Leontus said after a few moments, 'that no one is ever truly dead so long as they are remembered.'

'I like that,' Belgutei replied as he looked up to the heavens and pointed. 'Look, another shooting star.'

Arnetz appeared out of the darkness beside them at that moment, like a shadow slipping from the gloom with lasgun in hand.

'We found a dead Cadian on the waterside back there,' she said. 'Throat's been cut. Looked to me like she was one of Andersson's team who was watching the ambush site with him.'

'The orks must have followed her up to the plateau,' Leontus said. 'Any sign of Andersson or the others?'

'No, my lord.'

'Another one for us to remember,' Belgutei said.

They reached the first forward camp in the foothills just after daybreak, using the early morning mists to cover their passage through the narrow, twisting slot canyons to a deep recess beneath an overhang of dark stone.

The camp's sentries were ready and waiting for them a good distance from the camp itself; Arnetz's messengers had arrived in the night to forewarn them of the exodus from the plateau, and the possibility of ork activity nearby. Leontus was glad to see that they had taken the warnings so seriously, but it soon became apparent that the rocky overhang would be far too small to shelter them all.

'I could take a few squads to one of the other camps,' Arnetz offered as the troops unloaded the heavy bolter and its ammunition from Nomak's horse.

'It's too risky to move in daylight. We'll have to wait until nightfall,' Leontus said. 'Tell our people from the cavern to get some rest while they can.'

Leontus hitched Konstantin's reins to a spur of moss-covered stone and stepped out of the overhang's shadow and into the open daylight. The sun's warmth felt good on his skin, even if the sensation was somewhat offset by the gritty feeling in his eyes. God-Emperor above, he needed to sleep.

He lingered in the sunlight for a few more moments, his eyes closed as he tried to find some semblance of calm despite the concerns gnawing at his conscious mind. When he finally opened his eyes, it was to see a wisp of white cloud being teased apart by atmospheric winds. Darts of white light streaked behind it, disappearing behind the overhang as fast as they appeared.

Belgutei came to stand beside him and turned his eyes to the heavens as Leontus' mind worked.

'More shooting stars,' the Attilan said.

'They're not shooting stars.' Leontus smiled and made for where Arnetz was busy stowing the cavern's supplies.

'Arnetz, you said two days for the ork camp to reach the space port?'

'Yes, my lord,' Arnetz said, looking from Leontus to Belgutei in confusion.

'Good. You' – Leontus pointed to a Cadian wearing a corporal's stripes – 'your name, trooper?'

'Corporal Darneil, my lord.'

'Send messages to the other camps, Corporal Darneil. I want everyone to muster here tonight. At dawn tomorrow, we take the space port.'

FIFTEEN

Belgutei's first response was anger, tempered only by the warning look that Arnetz gave him as he shot to his feet.

'You knew that there were Attilans there and you didn't tell me?'

The Lord Solar didn't look away as Belgutei seethed, but Arnetz did.

'I am telling you now,' the Lord Solar said.

'It was only yesterday, Belgutei. As much as it feels like so much longer–'

'No,' Belgutei cut in, interrupting Arnetz. 'You should have said something. My people could be there.'

They were outside the camp, beyond the shadow of the overhang where the grass was still beaded with moisture, out of earshot of the rest of the troops. The Lord Solar sat on a low stone outcrop, whilst Arnetz stood with her back to the camp.

Belgutei paced in an attempt to cool the anger that fired

his blood. His rational mind knew that there had been good reason to keep the information from him, not least that Lord Solar and Arnetz hadn't had time to speak to him about the horses sighted in the ork camp. But none of that mattered, not if there was a chance that some of his people might still be alive.

'I promised to help find and liberate your people when the time was right. That time is coming,' the Lord Solar said.

'When do we leave?'

'Tonight, before dark.'

Arnetz watched as Belgutei stalked towards where Rugen and Csaba tended to the horses, hitched a short distance from where Konstantin stood.

'I hope that the Attilans are still alive. For their sake,' Arnetz said as the Lord Solar got to his feet.

'For all of our sakes',' the Lord Solar said. 'But I have another task for you.'

Despite the bone-deep fatigue and the tiredness that had seemingly poured sand under her eyelids, Arnetz found herself standing to attention beneath the Lord Solar's gaze.

'Yes, my lord?'

'I need you to lead the muster to the space port tonight. Begin the attack at dawn, regardless of whether I return with the Attilans or not – do you understand?'

Arnetz stared. 'My lord?'

'The others respect you. They will follow your orders until I return.'

'But… how? What plan should we follow?'

'We draw the orks out and fight our way inside.'

'Are… are you serious?'

'Entirely,' he said. 'It's the final step in the grand strategy,

Arnetz. It's everything that we have been building towards since the disaster at Bruke – we're drawing the orks in for the killing blow.'

'But the Attilans to the north-west–'

'If they still live, then I'll break them free to fight with us.'

Arnetz felt numb. She didn't fear battle; after all, she'd been brought up on a world that fought to kill her every day. But there was something final in the Lord Solar's tone that put her in mind of a gambler wagering everything on one last roll of the dice.

'Are you up to this, Arnetz?'

She thought of her squad – of Groger, Blasko and Strukker, killed at Bruke. She thought of Raust and Andersson, and the scores of men and women who lay dead and unburied across Fortuna Minor. They'd all given their lives trusting in one man's singular vision for victory, leading up to this one moment.

'I am, my lord.'

Hours later, as a handful of her men rode out with the Lord Solar and the Attilans, bouncing awkwardly as they clung to the Rough Riders' backs, she wondered if she would see any of them again.

A welcoming shout pulled her attention away from the riders as they passed out of sight, and she turned to see the first of the arrivals from the other forward operating bases making their way towards the camp.

She would have just shy of one hundred and fifty soldiers, according to the Lord Solar's count. That was a great weight of lives resting on her word; the Lord Solar might be used to commanding armies in their thousands, but as a medicae her experience was far more up close and personal.

'Squad leaders, assemble under the overhang,' she called as

yet more troopers filed into the narrow canyon. They would need to be briefed and organised if the Lord Solar's plan was to work. She would need to persuade them that this was possible, even as she doubted it herself.

With a final look at the darkening sky and the stars lancing across the horizon, she took a fortifying breath and made for the heart of the camp.

Belgutei fought the urge to push the pace on the ride northwest, not least because he had a burly Catachan sharing his saddle. The trails that led through the foothills were treacherous in the dark, and with only dim moonlight and the stars to guide them, their progress was painfully slow, at least in his mind. The thought that other Attilans may have survived on Fortuna Minor dominated his every thought, and it was hard to temper his hopes.

It took a few moments for him to orient himself when they finally emerged onto the plains west of the foothills. The space port was a blur of orange light on the southern horizon, its structures backlit by the fires of its xenos occupants.

'That must be the ork labour camp,' the Lord Solar said as he pointed to the west. An irregular constellation of lights danced in the darkness, less than an hour's ride away by Belgutei's judgement.

'Then we should go,' Belgutei said, but the Lord Solar held up a hand.

'Not until we have a plan,' he said, as still as his horse in the nimbus of low light that seemed to hang about him. 'These are your people and your terrain, Belgutei. What would you do?'

Belgutei almost laughed at the transparent attempt to coddle his ego, but he understood that the Lord Solar was right. He had spent his youth hunting on the open plains of Attila, living on horseback where the Lord Solar had not; Leontus was asking because Belgutei would likely have a good idea.

Belgutei grinned. 'The hawk and the vulture.'

Less than an hour later, when the ork camp was close enough that the creatures' gravelly, boisterous voices reverberated through the darkness, Belgutei called a halt and ordered the Catachans to dismount.

'Attack from the south once we engage,' he said as the death-worlders were swallowed by the darkness.

He turned his attention back to the ork camp, which was little more than a stationary convoy with no walls or defences. The xenos were gathered around a handful of promethium fires, charring hunks of bloody meat cut from a pair of horse carcasses lying at the camp's centre. The northern edge of the camp was dominated by a pair of massive sledges bearing huge metal plates, the firelight playing across a herd of ema-ciated horses resting in the sleds' shadow.

If the other Attilans still lived, then they must be nearby.

'Csaba, you are the vulture.'

Csaba nodded and kicked his horse forward in the direc-tion of the camp. Belgutei watched him cross into the light cast by the campfires in a rush of pounding hooves, his coat whipping behind him in the wind. The young Attilan let out his ancestral war cry as he urged his horse to greater speed, racing around the southern edge of the ork encampment and away into the darkness beyond.

The orks were on their feet with frightening speed – at least twenty of them as Arnetz had said, the largest wielding barbed whips and blunt-nosed firearms, which they emptied in Csaba's direction. Some gave chase, loping after the Attilan in a bow-legged charge as they bellowed in animalistic fury.

'That got their attention,' the Lord Solar said.

'The vulture circles, the hawk strikes,' Belgutei replied, drawing his sword as he kicked Nashi into a gallop. 'No lances, let them taste steel!'

Belgutei led Rugen and the Lord Solar into the orks' rear, their attention still on Csaba as the real attack struck.

They sliced through the disorganised xenos like light through the void, never slowing, their momentum carrying them through the camp in a blur of slashing swords and sundered meat. It was what Belgutei had been born for, and he revelled in the exhilaration of the kill.

Csaba rejoined them as they circled back for another pass, his sword in his hand and his features split in a wide grin. 'We are the wind, Belgutei!' he cried.

Las-fire lanced out of the darkness south of the encampment as Belgutei led the charging horsemen back towards the camp. The Catachans had chosen the perfect moment to strike, wrongfooting the orks as they tried to make sense of what was happening.

One of the xenos, a muscular beast at least a head taller than its savage kin, raised a brutal blade and roared, the sound impossibly loud and bestial in the darkness. It swatted one of the others aside, sending the smaller ork tumbling through the flames in a spray of embers as it charged southward towards the Catachans.

Belgutei planted his blade in its skull as he charged past, the sword torn from his grip in the meat of the ork's brain. It still turned to swipe at him, its vacant eyes unfocusing as it toppled to the dirt in a boneless heap.

The Lord Solar put down the last ork with a contemptuous swipe of Conquest, slicing off the top of the creature's head to reveal the greasy, blood-slicked meat of its brain.

'Attila! To me!' Belgutei screamed into the darkness on the northern edge of the camp, but there was no response. He left the others to finish the still-twitching xenos and headed towards the sleds, his handheld lumen illuminating his path in a cone of cold light.

The horses scrambled to stand as soon as they recognised one of their own, their bones standing proud beneath their taut skin. They still wore their saddles and hand-worked leather traces, the skin beneath rubbed raw by their long misuse, all bound into work gangs by lengths of blackened iron chain.

But they were not alone.

Men and women stepped out of the darkness between the horses, hollow cheeks and gaunt faces pale in the lumen's light as they held to their mounts for support. The tattered and torn scraps of armoured coats marked them out as Atti-lans, though the spiked collars and heavy chains were the closest they wore to uniforms under the orks.

Belgutei tried to speak, to offer warmth to these sorry shadows of once proud Rough Riders, but the words would not come.

'You have survived,' the Lord Solar said.

Belgutei turned, his attention so riveted on his people that he hadn't heard Konstantin's approach.

'We endured,' one man croaked in a dry, rasping voice, his skin an open weave of whip scars and fresh cuts.

'That is enough,' the Lord Solar said. 'Can you ride? Can you fight?'

The whipped man held up the chain that bound him to the sled and to his captured comrades. 'Free us and we will do both.'

SIXTEEN

Dawn broke over Fortuna Minor, setting the sky ablaze in hues of crimson and blazing orange as the system's distant star rose in the east. But for all its ephemeral beauty, the sunrise held little interest to Leontus as he rode south with his Attilans.

Once freed, the captives had plundered the ork camp for food and water, scavenging the tools they'd need for the fight ahead from the sleds they had dragged halfway across the continent. The horses looked little better than their riders, even invigorated as they were by the loss of their burden and being back in the hands of kinder masters.

'This is what would have awaited us had we run for the plains,' Belgutei had said as they'd broken the chains binding his people.

Leontus glanced to his right, where Belgutei rode by his side, lance in hand, his features resolute as the fortress loomed large in the distance. A column of figures could be seen to the south-east, making their way across the plains towards it in formations too organised to be of ork origin.

'Arnetz and the others,' Belgutei shouted over the hammering of hooves – eighteen horses riding at pace sounded like rolling thunder, adding a new layer to the intimidation they created on the charge.

'Hold here.' Leontus held up a hand to slow the riders to a halt, and turned to face his cavalry.

Fifteen Attilans and three Catachans stared back at him. The former captives sagged in their saddles, their fatigue beyond anything that Leontus could imagine, but they still clutched their improvised lances and held his gaze with grim determination.

Belgutei, Rugen, and Csaba had anger in their eyes. They exuded wrathful intent, as did the three Catachans who had taken the riderless horses from the ork camp; they weren't natural riders, but they would serve.

'This is where I leave you, for now,' Leontus said as the horses stomped and whickered at the sudden halt. 'Belgutei has command – follow his orders and fight hard. I will see you on the battlefield.'

Belgutei raised his lance in salute, his features a stoic mask as the other riders did the same.

'We will see you in the wind, Lord Solar.'

'That is a lot bigger up close,' Arnetz muttered.

The space port had become a ramshackle fortress under the orks' stewardship, its standard-pattern plascrete walls extended by blackened metal plating and scaffolds of scavenged scrap. Its gates were a hundred feet of mismatched steel and dull grey welds, overshadowed by tall towers that groaned precariously in the morning wind. The towers had been extended too, their supports gouged into the stone of the original gatehouse, the rusting metal spars leaving a dark orange stain on the pale plascrete below.

She called a halt as the Lord Solar rode into view from the north, his golden armour reflecting the dawn's cleansing light as it chased away both the darkness and any doubt that he might not return.

'Get into formation,' she shouted as the Lord Solar crossed in front of the space port. 'Follow your squad leaders, do your jobs, and we might just get through this.'

Figures moved in the ork guard towers; guttural calls were exchanged in the distance, followed by bellicose roars in a tongue she neither understood nor had to. The orks knew that the humans had come.

The Lord Solar looked every inch of the Imperial hero as he slowed Konstantin to a walk before his army, an icon of the Astra Militarum in gold and white. He nodded to Arnetz as he passed, his stony features set beneath the Radiant Helm as he surveyed his army.

Arnetz looked about her at the other survivors for the first time in the light, at the drawn faces of the one hundred and fifty Catachans and Cadians who had lived through the massacre at Bruke and so much more besides, all leading up to that moment. They could have run, or ignored the call to muster – but they had not. The Lord Solar had commanded, and so they obeyed.

'I have tasted fear before,' the Lord Solar called out, his voice carrying over the still air. 'I have tasted it and found it bitter and foul. The taste of victory is far sweeter. It is electrifying. It is addictive, and I will share it with you all today.'

He kicked Konstantin forward and turned to face his soldiers, the few survivors of a war that should have ended weeks ago. Arnetz stared back, her heartbeat rising to meet the rising chorus of voices from within the space port.

'I have fought beside demigods. I have knelt at the feet of a son of the God-Emperor Himself, but there is no one I would rather fight beside this day, against this enemy, because we owe them a debt. We owe them fire, and blood, and fury. We have survived a war that should have seen us dead on the first day, but still we fight on.'

Arnetz raised her chin, her jaw set and strong.

'Hold to your orders! Hold to your oaths! Fight on, unto victory and deliverance!'

The historitors would one day write that the soldiers had cheered his words, roaring their defiance in the face of impossible odds as the light of the God-Emperor suffused them with glorious purpose. But there were no propagandists on Fortuna Minor that day, and there was no cheering.

Instead, the gates began to grind open with the howl of a wounded leviathan, colossal engines belching smoke as the titanic plates parted to unleash the horde contained within. They washed forward in a roaring wave of battle cries and green flesh, their clan divisions forgotten as they swarmed from the fortress and out onto the plains.

The Lord Solar kicked Konstantin into a gallop, clearing the way for the heavy bolter and autocannon to start spitting death through the ork lines. The heavy bolter chattered in a staccato rhythm, its gunner pouring mass-reactive fire into the oncoming xenos in an unbroken stream. The autocannon's fire was slower but no less effective, its tracer rounds slicing deep into the mass of green flesh where the heavy bolter fire only put down the forerunners.

Dozens of orks were torn apart in the opening salvo, covering the retreat of the rest of the Lord Solar's infantry as they pulled back, putting more distance between themselves and the oncoming orks. The heavy weapons were abandoned as they clicked empty, their gunners sprinting back to rejoin their squads as the Lord Solar took up a position on the front rank.

Arnetz urged them on, readying her lasgun as the space port gates opened still wider, disgorging a growing stream of wild xenos fury.

'Grenades!'

The Lord Solar's order was quickly relayed through the ranks behind him by squad leaders and troopers alike. Arnetz added her voice to the shout more to have an outlet for her adrenaline as she faced down the incoming orks.

Then the first groups threw their grenades into the charge, falling back as their explosives sailed through the air. Each grenade detonated clouds of shrapnel and atomised ork flesh, but the xenos charged on through the droplets of bloody mist without hesitation.

'Open fire!'

The ranks of Astra Militarum responded as one to the Lord Solar's order. They all cut loose with their lasguns, emptying their weapons' charge packs in an unbroken stream of las-fire that scythed down the front ranks of the xenos charge, blunting the momentum long enough for the closest squads to fall back in a rolling retreat as the next squads opened fire.

Arnetz ordered her squad back with a curt shout, snapping off shot after shot as she followed, each organised withdrawal designed to pull the orks further out of the fortress like a splinter being teased from the skin.

The Lord Solar kept pace with the retreat as Konstantin backed away with mechanical movements that looked entirely at odds with his form.

Arnetz could only assume that the plan was working. But as she slapped a fresh charge pack into her lasgun and uttered a few words of the Litany of Reloading, she realised that she wouldn't have any idea that the plan had failed until it was too late.

Belgutei watched the orks stream from the space port in disgust. It was like watching maggots spilling free from a bloated corpse, a swarm of mindless parasites whose only impulse was pain.

'We should charge them now,' Csaba said from the horse beside him.

'Not yet,' Belgutei said, shaking his head. His eyes wandered to the Lord Solar. Leontus stood out from the patchy carpet of muted olive that were the Imperial forces, a shining bastion rising between the humans and the xenos baying for their blood.

The flow of orks between the gates was slowing but still hadn't stopped, despite the fearsome losses that their charge was taking.

The Lord Solar had been specific in his orders. The Attilans' time was coming, but not yet.

'Soon, Csaba,' Belgutei promised. 'The rest of you, ready yourselves.'

'Keep firing!' Leontus roared, Sol's Righteous Gaze hissing as its muzzle glowed from overuse. It was not an accurate weapon beyond short range, but it was almost impossible to miss the wall of flesh clawing its way to the Imperial lines.

He saw orks dying by the dozen under the weight of las-fire, their savage kin charging through clouds of atomised blood to smash the dead aside where they didn't fall fast enough, or else trampling their falling bodies underfoot.

'Fall back to the next position!' Leontus shouted.

Konstantin stumbled as the ground shook beneath his hooves, nearly throwing Leontus as the horse fought to right himself mid-step. It was almost time.

'Where is Belgutei?' Arnetz asked, her voice barely audible over the roar of the coming horde and the las-fire that couldn't hold them back. She dragged a soldier back to his feet as she raced to the next firing line, pushing him ahead of her as Leontus came alongside.

'He will come when we need him,' Leontus said.

The orks at the front started shooting as they ran, adding an arrhythmic chatter over the bass rumble of their running feet and their cries of rage. Bullets whined and fizzed overhead like so many angry insects, most shots slamming into the dirt well short of the Imperial lines. Those that did find flesh blasted the humans from their feet in sprays of blood and stringy meat, their bodies left where they lay with each rolling retreat.

The ground shook again, accompanied by a screech of tearing metal from within the fortress, audible even over the thunder of hundreds of orks and the ever-present crackle of las-fire.

'What in the name of the God-Emperor!?' someone shouted.

The flow of orks through the gates had slowed to a trickle, though those still emerging appeared to be running away from the walls rather than towards the enemy. A third ground-shaking thud revealed why.

A titanic shape bulled through the gates, smashing them apart with a swinging limb of rust-browned girders that ended in an immense three-pronged claw. The Gargant reached out and dragged the right-hand gate from its mountings and threw it aside with ponderous ease, crushing dozens of fleeing orks beneath tons of scrap iron and scavenged alloy.

The behemoth of ork insanity hauled itself through the space left by the ruined gates, a squat parody of the holy god-machines of the Adeptus Mechanicus. Its armour was a patchwork of hammered scrap and salvaged hull plating cut from the downed ship to the east, its chest dominated by a cluster of wide-bore cannons that wouldn't have looked out of place on a warship's cannonade deck. Its head was a pugnacious caricature of an ork's cavernous jaws and narrow forehead, perched on the monstrosity's shoulders between belching chimney stacks and rows of anti-aircraft guns.

It dragged itself forward on one working leg, the exposed machinery straining beneath the incomplete protection in its armour plating; it was far from finished, slowed down by Leontus' attacks on the ork convoys.

But it hadn't been stopped, as he had dared to hope.

'What are we supposed to do about that thing!?' Arnetz asked, her eyes flicking from Leontus to the walking building as it took another yawning step.

'There's nothing you can do – that's what the Attilans are for,' Leontus said, risking a glance to the north. There was no sign of Belgutei or his men, and the orks were almost at the Imperial lines.

'Keep drawing them out, Arnetz!' he called. Then, with a twitch of his reins, Konstantin leaped into forward motion like a bullet from a gun, leaving a trail of dust in his wake as Leontus turned his back on the battle and made off to the north.

Belgutei stared open-mouthed at the Gargant, which was a titanic metal edifice even from their position.

'Belgutei, what do we do?' Csaba asked.

The fear in the young man's eyes was a near-mirror of his own, only Csaba's was wild and unrestrained where Belgutei's had long since been broken. Belgutei looked to Rugen, who was impassive as ever, and the battered and beaten Attilans whom they had liberated just hours before.

None turned to flee. Not before this enemy.

'We kill it.' Belgutei smiled. 'Those of you without explosive lances are to protect those that do – we stay together on the charge, strike, and re-form until that thing is dead. Are you with me?'

The Attilans let out a shout of wordless affirmation. They were one, and they would be swifter than the wind.

Belgutei pressed his etched-bone hunting horn to his lips and blew a long, mournful note that stirred the blood of every Attilan. The horses started forward as one, gathering pace as they charged towards the titanic machine and the sea of green flesh that roiled in its shadow.

Riders jostled for position as the pace increased to a mile-eating gallop, those with improvised lances and weapons to the flanks and those with true hunting lances at the centre.

'The Lord Solar!' a Catachan shouted, pointing over to the south-east, where Leontus approached with unnatural speed, Konstantin's limbs moving faster than any true horse's could. He circled around and joined the charge, falling into position beside Belgutei.

'You knew about that thing, didn't you?' Belgutei said.

Leontus nodded. 'I suspected. The convoys and the ambushes were all to prevent that thing's completion.'

'And now it's complete?'

'That's why I have you.'

'Ha! You had this all planned from the start – even a few Rough Riders charging a Gargant!'

'More than a few,' Leontus said with a nod to the riders around them. 'I needed a swift hammer to break the back of our enemy. You are that hammer, Belgutei.'

'Barratt, fall back! First rank, open fire!'

Arnetz's voice was hoarse as she shouted her orders, both

from the constant cycle of fire-run-turn and fire again, and the stream of commands she gave to coordinate her squads. The orks were gaining rapidly and would eventually catch up with the rolling retreat, but that was to be expected. She would draw them on as far as she could before the ammunition ran out and all that remained was the dying.

The thought didn't scare her. She'd expected to die long before the assault on the space port, giving her life in one of the ambushes or in the attack on the downed ship.

Her lasgun cycled empty and she ejected the spent charge pack, allowing muscle memory to take over as she slapped a fresh one into place and readied the weapon to fire again, with a silent promise to honour the weapon properly if she got the chance.

The orks wouldn't stop. They couldn't stop. They were an endless tide, as undeniable as the wind or the oceans, a primal force that craved war as other races drank water or breathed air. The massive metal monstrosity that tore its way from the fortress was just another way that she might die, though it would likely be quicker than at the hands of the orks before her.

'Last charge pack!' someone yelled from beside her, a call that was repeated down the line as her own weapon emptied yet again.

'Fall back fifty yards!' she ordered, ejecting the spent charge pack and reaching for another, only to find her webbing empty. That was poor fire discipline on her part, and she laughed as she thought of what her old sergeant would have said had he been there to see it.

'You okay, sergeant?' a trooper asked as they ran back to the next position, past the volleys of las-fire from the squads to their flanks.

'I will be,' Arnetz said. She threw aside her empty lasgun as the squad turned to face the coming orks and the space port beyond, and drew her knife. 'I will be.'

Konstantin leaned into the charge, smashing orks from their feet with his golden armour and sculpted plasteel plating as Leontus lashed out with Conquest. Each blow clove through bone and flesh with equal ease, slicing the orks apart as he drove a brutal wedge through the stragglers around the Gargant's base.

It was killing by rote. Muscle memory allowed the weight of his blade to drag his arm down as it carved through his enemies. There was no feeling, no excitement, the elation that had once coursed through him on the charge long since drained away by the endless years of war and death.

The Attilans screamed battle cries and violent oaths as they followed along in his wake, putting their own swords to good use by cutting down the xenos that surged into the gaps left by their fallen brethren.

'How is that thing even standing?' Belgutei called to him.

Leontus had no answers to give. By every law of gravity and engineering he knew, the Gargant should have collapsed beneath its own weight with every halting, limping step it took. The skirt of armour plating that shielded one of its flanks bore the entire structure's weight as the exposed leg reached forward, the metal groaning with each lumbering movement. The leg was the key to halting the Gargant's advance, but it would mean riding into range of the walker's occupants and their primitive guns.

'Target the leg!' Leontus ordered.

The Gargant's chest-mounted cannons belched smoke and flame, rocking the entire structure back as the shockwave struck Leontus like a physical blow. The orks directly beneath the cannons were thrown from their feet by the force of it, the shells howling over the distant lines of humans to miss by dozens of yards. It was still close enough to shower them with powdered soil and dirt, and Leontus feared that the following shots could only land closer to their targets. With the gunlines gone, the orks would have but one target, and there would be no way to fight through them all to bring the Gargant down.

He kicked Konstantin into the charge, heading straight for the thick girders and heavy-jointed ironwork that made up the Gargant's foot. Solid rounds fizzed past him to chew up the earth by Konstantin's galloping hooves, several only turned aside by the refractor field built into his armour.

With ponderous slowness the foot began to lift, the super-structure shuddering as the entire weight of the Gargant settled on its armoured skirt. Leontus hissed in frustration as the Leman Russ-sized appendage lifted high above him, well out of the range of the Attilans' lances. Konstantin turned aside, curving away from the furnace-hot innards of the Gargant and back onto open ground, Belgutei's riders following in their wake.

But they didn't all escape unscathed. Horses screamed in pain behind him, and he turned to see riders tumbling to the dirt as their mounts collapsed beneath them. Some stayed where they had fallen, but one got unsteadily to his feet with a scavenged weapon in his hand, ready to meet the orks that converged on him.

Leontus looked around; he had eleven riders left.

'We attack again!'

He guided Konstantin through a long, sweeping turn back towards the Gargant, his eyes fixed on the behemoth's descending foot. He urged his mount to greater speed and leaned forward in the saddle, flashing wisps of lightning deflecting the gunfire that came too close, Conquest lancing out to strike down any orks that came within reach.

A Catachan rider fell to his right, pitched from his horse as a heavy-calibre round slammed into him with a wet thud. The horse charged on regardless, the spare lance in its saddle-bags dancing with each racing stride. Leontus reached out and slipped it free as he sped back into the shadow of the Gargant, trusting in his augmetic grip to hold the unwieldy weapon steady as the titanic foot descended.

He was prepared for the blast, but not the way that the lance twisted in his grip as it shattered. Pain flared in his shoulder as Konstantin galloped away, two more blasts following in quick succession as Belgutei and Csaba's lances detonated against the joint.

But still the Gargant stood tall, an unbroken monolith that towered over the battlefield.

Then its cannons fired again.

The shells whistled overhead towards the squads of infantry, who had finally been caught by the pursuing ork horde. Entire squads disappeared in a flash of fire and atomised earth, orks and humans alike swallowed by the blasts and hurled skyward in a boneless tumble that was sickening to watch.

Leontus looked away before they landed amidst the melee, turning back to see the Gargant's clawed foot rising for yet another step. Their lances had gouged still-glowing cavities in the thick metal, but seemingly not enough to break the machine's ponderous stride.

'Do we go again, my lord?' Belgutei asked, already fitting a new melta charge to the tip of his lance.

'We keep going until it's brought down.'

Arnetz swayed aside, evading a two-handed swipe from an ork's axe, ramming her knife through the creature's throat before it could bring its weapon around for another strike.

Ichor fountained from the wound in hot, stinking spurts, adding to the blood that already covered her arms up to the elbow.

There was no end to their number, no end to the biting and the clawing and the vicious swipes of brutal weapons. Each blow was a haymaker, their every sinew focused into delivering the strongest strike time after time, with no thought of finesse or technique. Arnetz fought smarter, refusing to match the orks' power as she attacked and faded, conserving what little energy she had left with an economy of movement.

It wasn't enough. The ground was muddy with mixed blood and ichor, the terrain beneath her feet uneven, as each step was as likely to land on the dead as the churned earth. She barely registered the shells that howled overhead from the Gargant, landing closer and closer each time. She'd caught sight of Barratt's squad in the periphery of her vision, disappearing in a flash of high-explosive, transformed from hardened fighters to ruined meat in the blink of an eye.

At least half of the Lord Solar's forces were lying dead or wounded around her, with more joining them with each passing second. She knew that thought should have troubled her, but it was abstract in that moment. It was another problem for someone else; all she had was the next enemy.

A scarred ork pushed through to her, a serrated metal plate where its lower jaw should have been, a shrieking chainaxe revving in its clawed hands.

'Come on then!' she roared, and leaped to the attack.

Leontus saw Rugen fall, the stoic Attilan meeting his death with his trademark impassive grace as his horse was cut down beneath him. He rolled to his feet, his sword in hand, as the other riders left him behind to circle around for another charge. Leontus saw him bury his sword in an ork's guts as the creature bit down on his neck, both combatants falling dead in an eternal embrace.

'Rugen is down!' Leontus shouted to the remaining six riders: Belgutei, Csaba, three emaciated Attilan Rough Riders, and a Catachan who still clung to his horse. Rugen had been a good man, a calm and considered influence on the others during their time in the cavern, and Leontus felt a surprising pang of loss at his passing.

'I know,' Belgutei said, throwing aside what remained of his lance as he rode alongside Leontus. 'He rides by the God-Emperor's side now.'

'We need one more pass,' Leontus said through gritted teeth. The Gargant's foot was stained purple and yellow with heat bloom, the ankle joint burned half through by the last of their melta charges.

'We're out of lances and explosives,' Belgutei said, 'and I doubt that our lasguns will do much against it.'

'They won't, but this might,' Leontus said, drawing Sol's Righteous Gaze. 'I'll need to get in close, and it will take more than one shot.'

'I understand. Riders, protect the Lord Solar!'

Belgutei turned, his power sword raised as he signalled the final charge. The others formed up in a protective circle around the Lord Solar, shielding him from the orks with their own bodies on the churned ground between them and the Gargant.

Csaba was the first to fall, smashed from his saddle by an ork's axe that he couldn't avoid.

One of the rescued Attilans fell next, his thin body peppered with gunshots as they passed beneath the Gargant's armour and within range of its crew.

'Give me as much time as you can!' Leontus shouted to the

others, knowing that each shot would be bought with their blood.

Sol's Righteous Gaze barked repeatedly, each pull of the pistol's trigger blasting fist-sized glowing holes in the metal superstructure. The punishing heat within the Gargant was oppressive, but nothing to the heat Sol's Righteous Gaze gave off as Leontus hammered shot after shot into the walker's ankle.

But the power of cavalry was its speed – an essential asset that they had been forced to abandon to bring down the Gargant. The orks, in all their ferocity, didn't allow the opportunity to pass them by.

The creatures poured gunfire down on the riders below, heedless of whether their uncontrolled sprays hit the humans or the xenos that flooded into the Gargant's sweltering innards after the horsemen that had escaped them for so long.

The last Catachan cried out in pain as he was dragged from his horse by taloned claws and set upon with savage fury, his agonised screams only driving the orks on to greater violence. Bloodstained xenos scrambled over his screaming steed to get at the Attilans, who wheeled their mounts in an attempt to hold back the press even as bullets churned the earth beneath them.

Still Leontus fired, the muzzle of his pistol lost beneath a heat haze, the white leather of his gloves blackening from each shot's unshielded backwash.

'My lord!' Belgutei shouted, and Leontus glanced away from his target for a heart-stopping moment.

Belgutei was drenched in blood, both ork and his own, his sword steaming as the power field burned off the sticky ichor. Nashi was stumbling beneath him, holding him above the fray despite half a dozen wounds that seeped bright blood over her flanks. He was the Lord Solar's last defender; Leontus realised that the Attilan hadn't called out for help, but to warn him that he would shortly be alone.

With a last, grim smile, Belgutei hacked at the orks clamouring for his flesh and fell out of Leontus' sight.

Leontus turned back to the Gargant's descending leg, Sol's Righteous Gaze smoking in his hand and his glove completely blackened below the wrist. He raised the pistol once more and fired more metal-chewing shots into the slagged metal of the gigantic ankle, punctuating each shot with a silent prayer for the God-Emperor's favour.

The tank-sized foot hammered into the earth, but this time the leg above it kept moving, shearing through the weak point drilled into the thick metal limb. The full weight of the Gargant wasn't lowered onto the armoured skirt but slammed into it, countless tons of cannons, ordnance, armour, and machinery all compressed into an unexpected impact.

With a moan of tortured metal the armoured skirt crumpled, sending the Gargant forward into an unrecoverable lean.

Inside the Gargant, Leontus was showered with rivets as the interior structures collapsed beneath their own weight. He kicked Konstantin forward, the horse almost having to wade through the fleeing xenos as they clamoured to escape the shrieking metal construct.

Some of the orks outside the Gargant looked up as it loomed over them, suddenly aware of their impending doom as if it had been subconsciously broadcast to them. Others still fought to get at the humans, unaware of the thousands of tons of mechanical death that would grind them to paste beneath its weight. Those that were aware began to run, abandoning the battle in a vain attempt to survive, but their massed numbers held them in place.

The Gargant collapsed in a cataclysmic impact; it was as if the world itself was ending, rent apart by the titanic boom of the behemoth's weight as it kicked up a cloud of dust that consumed everything in its path. Orks died by the score, blinded by dirt and pulverised beneath the Gargant's bulk as its head rolled from its shoulders and broke against the bloody earth.

Leontus fell blindly, thrown from Konstantin's back by the impact, and met the ground with hammering force.

SEVENTEEN

Arnetz dragged her knife clear of the ork's eye socket, coughing in the cloud of dust raised by the Gargant's fall. Her own blood mingled with the thick paste of ork ichor on her arms and shoulders, dripping from her broken nose to spray out with each hacking breath.

She used the momentary break in the melee to pick up a discarded lasgun. Breathlessly, she checked the charge and thanked the God-Emperor that it was still half full.

'Form up on me!' she shouted into the settling dust cloud.

A handful of her people rallied to her side, some clutching battered lasguns, the others reduced to wielding hand weapons. Every single one was bruised and bleeding.

'We can use this – we make for the space port.' Arnetz pointed to the spire, only just visible through the dust cloud.

A dazed ork lurched into sight, its skin covered in a crust

of ochre powder. Arnetz shot it dead before it could take another step.

'We move.'

Leontus pushed himself to his feet, his left hand still clutching Sol's Righteous Gaze; the augmetic had seized around the pistol's grip, and he found that he was unable to release the still-glowing weapon.

He stumbled forward through the settling dust. There was no way to orient himself, no landmarks that he could see other than the slumped mountain of the Gargant, so he kept it to his right as he searched for any sign of non-xenos life.

A hatch fell free of the Gargant's hull a few yards ahead, followed by a heavily augmented form tangled in lengths of rubber hosing and segmented cables. The 'Ead Nobz struggled to regain his feet as Leontus approached, though the number of heads dangling at the ork's waist was much diminished by the fall. Black ichor seeped from the holes in his scalp where the cables had been torn out, and dripped from the metal dreadlocks that had lost their suspended heads.

He turned as he heard Leontus' approach, planting a clawed hand on the Gargant's hull to steady himself. The other grasped a bundle of rubberised cables and segmented metal cords like a flail, the slack-mouthed heads scraping in the dirt as their eyes stared vacantly across the plains.

Leontus raised Sol's Righteous Gaze to shoot, but the augmetic wouldn't obey. The threat was enough to make the 'Ead Nobz freeze in place, however.

'You did dat,' he grunted accusingly, jerking his head at the fallen Gargant.

'We did,' Leontus said. He tried to pull his pistol's trigger, but the augmetic was entirely seized, reduced to unfeeling metal on the end of his arm.

'You krumped a Gargant…' the beast continued, thinking aloud, his eyes glassy as he spoke. 'If we kills you, den we krumped a Gargant.'

'Is that how it works for your kind?' Leontus asked. The 'Ead Nobz shrugged, then drew and fired his pistol in one lurching movement.

There was no time for Leontus to move or defend himself before the bolt of white light slammed into the centre of his breastplate, blowing out his helm's refractor field in a flash of flickering sparks. The Lord Solar staggered back and dropped to one knee, rolling aside as the 'Ead Nobz brought his flail down with a sickening crunch of bone and smashing glass.

Conquest's power field flared into life just in time to catch the next swing of the flail, cutting neatly through the cords and cables to scatter the severed heads across the ground nearby. The 'Ead Nobz dropped the weapon's useless remains and activated the narthecium gauntlet's howling drills, bringing the cutting edges down on Leontus' seized augmetic. The Lord Solar's hand fell limp, dropping Sol's Righteous Gaze to the ground, where the dirt blackened around its barrel.

Unbowed, Leontus drove the 'Ead Nobz back with wide, heavy swings of Conquest, the power field crackling as it singed the rubber hoses dangling from the ork's skull, before bringing the sword down in an overhand strike that the 'Ead Nobz leaped back to avoid. Then he took a step away and deactivated Conquest, driving it blade-down into the ground.

'You'z gonna fight me proppa, den?' the 'Ead Nobz said, smiling.

'Not exactly,' Leontus said, scooping up Sol's Righteous Gaze with his working hand.

He fired it twice, blasting off the ork's arms before the beast could take another step towards him. With a third shot, he blew away the 'Ead Nobz's augmetic leg in a spray of slagged metal, and the ork finally fell to the ground with a howl of pain and impotent rage. Leontus holstered Sol's Righteous Gaze and regathered Conquest, bringing the blade to rest against the xenos' throat.

'You'z a good nemesis,' the ork grunted between pained breaths, his blood spilling out in rhythmic spurts from his ruined arms. 'I chose good, I did.'

'I was the greatest threat you ever faced, beast,' Leontus said through gritted teeth, then he leaned in close. 'But to the Imperium, you were just another ork.'

Conquest's power field flared once more and sliced through cables, bone, and sinew to sever the creature's head in one sure stroke. The 'Ead Nobz's jaws worked as he mouthed unspeakable curses, the few remaining mummified heads still gnashing and snarling silently despite the death of their host.

'Lord Solar?' Arnetz said.

Leontus' head jerked up, taking in the bloodied Catachan and the handful of equally battered troopers behind her. He could hear orks rousing nearby, regrouping for the inevitable slaughter, but he didn't plan on waiting around for that.

'Come on. We should make for the fortress before the orks return.'

They headed for the space port at a run, only stopping to collect Konstantin when the Lord Solar found him near the Gargant's base. The plating around the horse's flanks and neck were gouged and dented, his armoured filigree caked in bloody mud, but he appeared otherwise unhurt as the Lord Solar stepped back into the saddle.

Mercifully, the majority of the orks were still lost in the settling dust on the other side of the fallen Gargant, but they didn't run unopposed.

'Another three on our right!' Arnetz called out as her lasgun clicked empty. She reversed her grip on the weapon and used it as a club to smash aside a wounded ork, the other two falling to shots from her squad.

'They'll have heard that – keep moving,' the Lord Solar said.

The Lord Solar was the first through the titanic gates that led into the fortress, his pistol held ready as he surveyed the devastation left in the wake of the orks' long tenancy. Grots scattered at the humans' approach, the last guardians of the space port who had been too scared to charge out alongside their larger kin. They were little threat so long as they didn't get too close, and it didn't seem like they had any intention of allowing that to happen.

'Check the hangars for a ship, anything that'll get us out of here,' Arnetz said to one of the other survivors, but the Lord Solar held up a hand to stop them.

'There will be nothing usable left. The orks have held this place for too long.'

'My lord?' Arnetz asked, a note of desperation entering her voice. 'If there are no ships… Why are we here?'

She was so damned tired. The Lord Solar had said that the space port would be their deliverance, but even that seemed to be slipping out of her reach.

The first of the orks came through the gates at a run, hefting a two-handed axe in its massive hands as it spotted the humans. It took three shots for her squad to put it down, which emptied one of their few remaining lasguns.

'Find weapons that we can use, quickly!' Arnetz said as other heavy-shouldered forms charged into the space port.

'We are here because of the bigger picture,' the Lord Solar said. 'The mission never changed, Sergeant Arnetz. I came to Fortuna Minor to cleanse it of the ork menace. That is what we are doing.'

Two more orks fell before they could reach the humans; the third launched itself at the Lord Solar and received a shot from Sol's Righteous Gaze in return.

More were coming, and it sounded like they weren't alone. The thrum of distant engines was just audible above the baritone growl of their voices, jet engines that doubtlessly belonged to ork aircraft. The Lord Solar just sat there as if waiting for the inevitable to come, but Arnetz couldn't do that. Not after all that she'd survived on this God-Emperor forsaken world.

'We need to find a defensible position,' Arnetz said to the other survivors as the Lord Solar looked skyward. 'Hurry!'

'You have my position?' the Lord Solar said to himself. 'Good. We have drawn them together. Enemy approaching from the east in force. Deal with it before extraction.'

'My lord, who are you talking to?' Arnetz asked. 'Please, we need to find somewhere–'

Three jet-powered aircraft howled overhead at supersonic speed, drowning out her words in their thunderous backwash. Arnetz ducked, waiting for the inevitable blast of dropped bombs or gunfire that would follow as the ork aircraft zeroed in on them.

But the bombs and bullets didn't fall, at least not within the fortress.

The plains around the Gargant's carcass were washed with cleansing fire that consumed the returning orks and their fallen god-machine. More jet-powered aircraft criss-crossed the skies to the east in strafing runs, but not in the telltale red of ork Speed Freeks: they bore the tan-and-blue livery of the Imperial Navy.

'Understood, fleetmaster,' the Lord Solar said over the thump of falling bombs, casting about himself to take in the other survivors. 'We have six for extraction. No, I will remain planet-side to coordinate the rest of the campaign.'

A Valkyrie swooped in low overhead, black rappelling lines dropping from its open hatches as a squad of Tempestus Scions slid down to the ground. Their metallic blue armour gleamed in the sunlight, and their leader made straight for the Lord Solar as the Valkyrie peeled away to add its weapons to the attack.

'Lord Solar,' the Scion said with a crisp salute, their face hidden behind a respirator mask and emerald lenses. 'Captain Kohaine. My men and I are at your disposal.'

More Valkyries flew in low, slowing to a hover as their troops disembarked before screaming skyward again in a wash of heat and sound that was all but deafening to Arnetz.

She couldn't believe the sight before her eyes – there were other humans on Fortuna Minor. The fleet had returned with reinforcements, just as the Lord Solar had said they would.

'Captain, secure the perimeter. I want a mile-wide cordon in every direction – this is where we land the armies,' Leontus said. 'What is the situation in orbit?'

The Lord Solar pressed a hand to the side of his helm, the motion an exact imitation of how her long-dead squadmate, Blasko, had used to listen to communications over the vox. Arnetz realised that the Radiant Helm must have some subtle workings built into its intricate design that included a vox, and the aircraft screaming overhead were providing a usable link to the ships in orbit.

A Scion took hold of Arnetz's arm and steered her away

from the Lord Solar and towards a Valkyrie that had landed nearby. The other survivors were also being escorted to the aircraft, one being all but carried by the Scion supporting him.

Arnetz allowed herself to be pushed onto the flyer, where a white-coated chirurgeon gently but firmly peeled her fingers from her knife and set it aside, promising that it would be returned as soon as they reached the fleet.

Her last sight of the Lord Solar was of him sitting astride Konstantin, directing the second invasion of Fortuna Minor as the Valkyrie doors slid closed. As the engines' pitch rose to a deafening scream, Arnetz allowed herself to relax as the chirurgeons set to work, and slipped into a dreamless sleep.

EPILOGUE

The doors to his private chambers closed behind him with a whisper of airtight seals, leaving Leontus alone at last.

He let out a long-held breath and allowed his head to drop onto his chest, reaching up with his free hand to unclasp the Radiant Helm and slip it from his head with a satisfied sigh. His neck ached abominably from the weight; he'd been wearing it for too long, and his body was telling him so.

Far too long.

Crystal-globed lumens suffused the passage ahead with soft, warm light, illuminating the wood panelled walls of his chambers aboard the *Lux Vindicta*, and the items mounted on them.

His spaceborne sanctum, a home far from home.

He moved down the carpeted floor past arms and armour mounted between the lumens, each item displayed with the deference due to its former owner. Cracked Cadian flak armour was displayed beside a Valhallan ushanka; a Kasrkin's battered shoulder guard beside a scorched Tempestus Scion's beret; a Krieg gas mask with a shattered eye-lens beside a fragment from a Cochlerati Janissary's armour.

On and on the artefacts went as he walked, lining almost every inch of his chambers' walls with the detritus of a lifetime's battlefields, until he reached an empty space beneath a broken Catachan knife and a Praetorian's pith helmet.

Leontus hefted the long, thin package in his hand, shaking loose the canvas wrappings to reveal the remains of an Attilan hunting lance. The grip was worn smooth by long use, the shape of the former owner's hand forever imprinted on the dark wood.

With a care that bordered on reverence, Leontus raised the broken lance and laid its weight on two awaiting mounts set into the wall, then placed his hand gently on the charred haft.

'Thank you, Belgutei.'

ABOUT THE AUTHOR

Rob Young is a writer and graphic designer from Lancashire whose work for Black Library includes the novels *Longshot* and *Leontus: Lord Solar,* and the short stories 'The Roar of the Void' and 'Transplants'.

THE LION: SON OF THE FOREST
by Mike Brooks

The Lion. Son of the Emperor, brother of demigods and primarch of the Dark Angels. Awakened. Returned. And yet… lost.

YOUR
NEXT READ

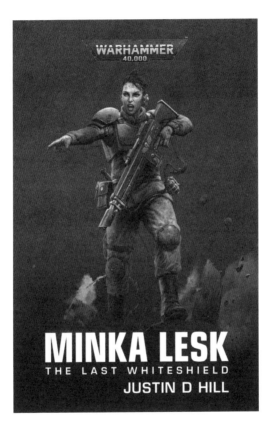

MINKA LESK: THE LAST WHITESHIELD
by Justin D Hill

Cadia has stood in grim defiance against the enemies of the Imperium for ten thousand years, an indomitable bulwark against the forces of Chaos… but now, the 13th Black Crusade has come, and there will be no victory. Here, Minka Lesk will be tested in the very fires of a world's destruction.

ENJOYED THE STORY?
RECREATE IT IN MINIATURE!
WARHAMMER 40,000
Get started at Warhammer40000.com